My Name is Sam…

And Heaven is Still Shining Through

1

Joe Siccardi

Higher Ground Books & Media

Springfield, Ohio.

http://www.highergroundbooksandmedia.com

Printed in the United States of America 2019

Foreword

The morning sky is dark with rolling clouds as I sit on a boardwalk bench in Seaside Heights, NJ, just reflecting about how blessed my life has been. The waves are anxious, pounding the pristine sand in a precise, rapid rhythm. The boardwalk is empty except for a few early morning gulls and a man standing by the rail about 100 feet away. As I huddle here, I close my eyes, soaking in the sounds of the surf, the fresh, clean smell of the air, the feel of the salt air enveloping me in the gentle breeze.

Through the veil I sense the clouds suddenly open. When I opened my eyes, I could see the gray sky punctuated by shades of morning pink and blue with a pure white center. You can't see the sun but know it is just behind that one puffy, thin cloud. Rays shoot out in all directions.

Immediately my thoughts dart to my early Religion class days and something my Daddy said.

Sister Mary Louise was teaching us about Noah's Ark. She emphasized God's love for us as symbolized in a rainbow. She told us whenever we saw a rainbow, we should say a little prayer and thank God for loving us and keeping His promises. The class created individual rainbows on craft paper. I remember mine was far from perfectly arched with the colored crayons overlapping.

But I was proud of my six-year-old creation and couldn't wait to show it to Mom and Daddy. Mom politely told me it was "beautiful." Daddy peeked at it while driving and told me I did a good job. Then he said, "We might see a rainbow" since the clouds were dark and it was raining.

We didn't see a rainbow that day, but Daddy spotted the sun trying to peek through the clouds and pulled the old Plymouth over so we could observe. You couldn't see the sun but knew it was just behind that one puffy, thin cloud. Rays shot out in all directions.

"Wow!" I said.

"Isn't that amazing?" answered Dad.

"Yes, dear," said Mom.

"Look at how it sparkles," I added.

"Do you know what that is?" asked Dad. As I was shaking my head no, he said, "That's heaven shining through."

"You mean God is doing that?"

"You betcha."

From that moment, the sun's rays became my symbol of hope. It didn't replace the rainbow but supplemented it. Whenever I was challenged or feeling down, God would allow heaven to shine through to remind me of His presence. Yes, even in those days when I was trying to ignore Him, God's light shone through.

I did have a good life. An ordinary life, yes, but good. No "ah hah!" moment, just a string of "ahs" weaving a tale of life, love, loss, some sorrow, but oh so much joy!

That is my life. I recognize some drama, some humor, some heart tugs. I know because I lived it. Just a free-willed suburban Jersey girl trying to figure out this journey called life.

So, today I lean back and continue to breathe in the saltwater and feel the sun on my face, constantly reminded of God's presence in the ordinary as He allows heaven to shine through.

Love,
　Sam

Chapter One

The Mustang muscled its way through the early mid-May night, each twist and turn on the northern New Jersey back roads to Greenwood Lake, NY, responsive to my touch. It was 1966. The top was down, allowing the humid air to whip around the car and its occupants. The radio was turned all the way up, fighting the outside noise with music of the night. The four of us were already screaming to be heard – occasionally punctuated with off-key singing – screeching, actually – when Cousin Brucie picked a relevant platter to play.

My name is Samantha – although everyone calls me Sam. I'm the captain of this ship, keeping an ever-vigilant eye on the road for wayward animals while deftly interacting with my crew and passengers.

Bernie – Mary Bernadette, my longest and dearest best friend – was my navigator, also sharing road awareness duties with good but loud conversation. In the back were Betty and Lynn. The four of us went through Mary Help of Christians Academy and were known as the Fearsome Foursome. There were five of us in the pack. Pat joined us on our weekend adventures, although she went to Passaic Valley and in the year since graduating high school, she moved to Rochester, NY.

Bernie and I had been together since the fourth grade back at St. Anthony's. Betty joined the "crew" in the sixth grade and Lynn started tagging along when we were freshmen. We all had empathy – but Bernie sometimes lacked tact. We weren't mean girls – okay, maybe sometimes, but only when others were being jerks.

I guess you could say Bernie and I were the leaders of our pack, but for decidedly different reasons. The difference between us was I was more diplomatic and tried to use reason with others, although I admittedly did have a sarcastic streak. When you irritated Bernie, on the other hand, it was like getting hit in the back of the head with a beer bottle.

Betty and Lynn were the followers. Both were less secure with themselves. More often than not, they would dump their problems on me rather than dealing with Bernie's off-the-cuff caustic snipes. But we all knew under that tough exterior was a heart of gold. And we all knew if we called her at three in the morning, she would be there for us. Actually, all of us would for each other – no questions asked. We were that tight.

I knew the outing tonight was going to be special ... bittersweet but special. It was the first time the four of us had gotten together since late last summer when our lives changed and took on different trajectories. I could see it already with Lynn who sort of floundered in the almost a year since we flipped our tassels. Since she was around, I sensed her displeasure with life in general and college in particular. We had many conversations – many, many conversations – as we commiserated about our respective first year college experiences. Bernie was usually involved when we got together on weekends, but since she was working in the "real world" she couldn't relate in the same way.

Betty also seemed different. She appeared to have more confidence overall, although, even on the short ride, I could sense she fell back into the scholastic pecking order.

Bernie was ... well, Bernie, perhaps a tad more jaded than when we roamed the halls of Mary Help of Christians.

We were celebrating Betty's return from Miami and Lynn's 18th birthday. We headed to Greenwood Lake since New York's drinking age was 18 back in the mid-60s.

Even though we all started working last summer – I worked at the local bakery – whenever we had the chance, we were together. It wasn't unusual for us to just take off for the Jersey Shore. Coyly watching and teasing boys on the boardwalk at Seaside Heights was a staple of the summer, which raced by too quickly. Soon enough, it came time to say a tearful good-bye to Betty as she headed to the Sunshine State and the University of Miami. Although Bernie and Lynn stayed around – Bernie went to cosmetology school and the workplace while Lynn attended Fairleigh Dickinson University – I knew life was changing and would never be the same, but I was determined to savor every minute.

I maneuvered the car into the parking lot at Mother's Bar on the New York side of the lake. I put the convertible top up as the girls adjusted their hair and makeup in the side view mirrors.

"Okay girls. Here we go. It's ladies night out. Let's have some fun!" I commanded amid a cacophony of laughter.

Chapter Two

We were escorted to a table near the dance floor, spotting groups of guys as we walked in. I made eye contact with a good-looking guy in the corner, but quickly looked away. The other girls spotted him, too, leading to snickers and arm pokes and an occasional look back.

The waitress arrived, "Welcome" she said above the din of the music. "Girls night out?"

"You got it!" I answered, "We're back together after a long, long year apart."

"Great. Let me see some IDs and we'll get this party started."

As I handed over my license, I quipped, "We're celebrating Lynn's birthday …"

Lynn interrupted, "And yours!"

"Yeah, mine too, but I'm older than you are."

"I'm glad to be back from Miami," added Betty.

Bernie chimed in, "And I'm here for the ride."

"Okay," said the waitress with pen and paper in hand. "What can I get you?"

I answered first. "I'll have a rum and Coke" with Bernie quickly behind me, "A beer."

Lynn interrupted, "A beer? Couldn't you be more creative?"

"Well, what are you going to get?" countered Bernie.

"I don't know yet. What about you Bet?"

"I don't know either."

"Come on girls," I interjected.

Betty asked if they had daiquiris. "I'm sure we do," answered the waitress. "Yeah, strawberry daiquiri. I'll have a strawberry daiquiri." Lynn echoed, "Me too." That prompted Bernie to ask, "Geez. Do you two even know what a daiquiri is?"

With a smile and light laugh, I shook my head and said, "Let them go. It's party time."

"I'll put your order in. Have fun," said the waitress.

As we scanned the room, heads bobbing with the live music, our drinks arrived.

"So, Betty, how was Miami?" I asked.

"It was okay. I mean, I did okay".

"Lots of cute boys?" asked Lynn, causing Bernie to add a caustic "Really?"

Betty responded, "Yeah, there were a lot of cute boys. Just not too many my type."

"Oh, what's your type?" asked Bernie.

"Well, you know, I like them cute, but most of the guys there were so … self-centered. All they thought about was themselves."

Betty wasn't off the hook. Lynn pressed her, "So? Did you go out on a lot of dates?"

"I went out on some, but you know, I should be the center of attention, right Sam?"

I almost choked on my drink. "Why are you asking me?"

"Duh," responded Bernie, "Because you're always the center of attention. Guys flock to you. You're a guy magnet."

Shaking my head, I answered, "You must be thinking of a different Sam."

"Oh yeah? Anyone here go to a prom? Raise your hand," said Betty. No one raised their hand, but Betty to my left and Bernie to my right grabbed my arms and hoisted them into the air.

"Let's see," mused Betty. "Two hands … and they both belong to … you!"

I couldn't think of an immediate rebuttal.

"Okay, so I went to two proms," I finally muttered. "So what?"

"Nobody else did," said Lynn. "You were the belle of the ball, not once but twice. Pray, milady, tell us about them."

"You know the stories," I said. "I don't have to repeat them."

"Yes you do," they insisted.

"Well, they weren't exactly the best nights of my life," I answered, putting on a sly smile, "although they weren't that bad either."

"Who was the first one with?" asked Betty.

Shaking my head, I answered, "Lenny, but …"

"Lenny. He was that kid from Central who had a crush on you, right?"

"I don't know if he had a crush on me. I mean he was a family friend. Went to his senior prom, he joined the Navy and we haven't seen each other since."

"And then there was …" prompted Lynn.

"John."

"Yeah, John," said Bernie. "He was quite a character."

I chuckled as I recalled my memories of John. He went to Passaic Valley and was one of Pat's friends. She actually talked me into going to the prom with him.

"We dated a couple of times after the prom," I said, "but you guys remember he was a nut job."

"Refresh our memories," asked Betty. "Didn't he leave you stranded?"

"Okay, he was, well, clingy. You all know the story. We went to Palisades one night and rode the Tunnel of Love. I wasn't in an amorous mood …"

"You!" said Lynn.

"… long story short, he was so we got into a big fight. Next thing I knew the sonfabitch was gone. Left me there, right at the amusement park."

"Aaand," prompted Betty.

"And what. Good thing I had a few dollars tucked in my shoe …"

"I taught her that trick," interjected Bernie.

"I ended up taking a bus back home."

"But that's not the best part of the story," said Bernie.

"I wouldn't call what happened later as the best part. I would call it the sad part."

"So, what happened next?" pressed Betty, although all three of them knew the story.

"A couple of days later he called me to apologize …"

"She wouldn't even talk to him," said Bernie.

"Are you telling the story or am I?" I asked.

"I'll finish it. It was Sam at her best," said Bernie. "So John keeps calling, but Sam won't talk to him. This went on for a couple of days. I was with her on Saturday morning when he called – again – but she wouldn't budge."

"Why should I? He left me at the amusement park! He didn't know I had money to get home. He just didn't care," I protested.

"Whatever," said Bernie. "Saturday night she gets a frantic call from Pat. John's sister called her and said John locked himself in his room and said he was going to kill himself because Sam wouldn't talk to him. So we end up going to his house so Sam could calm him down."

"I don't think he would have done anything. He was too chicken shit," I said. "I talked to him and told him why I was mad at him. He didn't think he did anything wrong! I told him it was wrong and made him promise he would never do that to another girl … ever!"

Bernie continued, "Bottom line is they talked for about an hour and a half …"

"And life went on," I added, "without John."

"The moral of the story," Bernie said, "is how much influence Sam has over guys. She can wrap them around her finger, and they never know what hit them."

"You're exaggerating," I said. "Besides, you guys all knew the story. How many times have we talked about it? A hundred?"

"No, only once," said Lynn. "You told us about John leaving you at Palisades, but you never told us about saving his life."

"I didn't save his life. I just talked him through a rough spot. It isn't something you just blurt out," I said, glaring at Bernie. "Why would you even bring that up?"

"Because you're our hero," said Betty. "You're just so smooth with the guys," said Lynn.

"Come on," I said, "we've all had dates from hell."

"But you, my friend," offered Bernie, "you know how to handle them. That's what makes you so special!"

All I could do was shake my head.

Changing the subject, Betty asked me, "Did you ace all your classes as usual Miss Brainiac?"

"Yeah, right," I responded. "I was lucky to get through the year."

"That must have made your Mom happy," tagged Betty.

"Oh yeah. You know Mom. Never good enough. This year I really gave her something to complain about," as I broke into a wide smile. "And did she complain!"

"She did," said Bernie, "but Miss Congeniality got even. She went out every weekend and raised hell!"

"What about you Bern?" asked Betty, trying to catch up first hand on the last nine months.

"I'm working. I have a chair at a salon in Wayne."

"Exciting," said Betty. "What about you Lynn?"

"I finished the year at Fairleigh Dickenson, but I don't think I'm going back. I'm supposed to start working at my Dad's place next week as a receptionist. If I like it, I might just take some time off from school."

I contributed, "I know. I heard all about it. I've been trying to talk some sense into her. Her Mom and Dad think it's my fault she doesn't want to go back to school."

Bernie added, "And I got some of the blame, too. Her parents thought Sam and I were too close to her and a bad influence. Go figure!"

Feigning shock, Betty animatedly said, "You guys?"

"Did you hang out a lot during the year?" Betty asked.

"We usually would find something to do on weekends," I answered.

"I missed that," said Betty. "Hanging out with you guys. Most of the girls in Florida were snobs. If you didn't belong to a sorority you were an outcast. And they were so catty."

"Come on," said Lynn. "I'm sure you had friends. What about your roommate?"

"Kathy? We never really clicked. She was okay, but she wasn't like you guys. We didn't fight or anything but just had different interests. She was on the cheerleading squad and always had dates. I stayed in the room and actually studied."

"Get out of town," said Bernie, her hand slapping the table. "You? Study? I don't believe it. We've been friends too long. None of us ever studied."

"No, really, I did. I had a 3.2 GPA," answered Betty

Lynn contributed, "Mine was 2.6," to which I replied, "That's about where mine was."

A quiet came to the table. The girls – well not Bernie because she knew me so well – couldn't believe an academic star could drop that low.

It was then, during that interchange, my worst friendship fears were realized. We were having a conversation, but it was more small talk. It lacked the gusto and swagger we commanded at MHC. We would randomly blurt out an irrelevant fact and just go with it for hours. We had our own "code" – mostly revolving around guys. We never would have talked about grades and about the only time academics would be interjected into the conversation was when we talked about a specific test. Even then, it was just a short interlude.

Yeah, we had changed just over the last nine months. We went from the Fearless Foursome to four young women trying to figure out our respective places in this world. I recognized the shift and, quite frankly, wasn't as happy looking forward as I was looking back.

Chapter Three

We again surveyed the club, this time a little more sedately although bobbing to the soulful rendition of The Mamas and The Papas' *Monday, Monday* by one of the in-house bands. All of a sudden, this guy came to our table.

"Hi girls. My name is Jimmy." Then looking straight at me, he asks, "Would you care to dance?"

He actually caught me off guard. Normally, checking out and interacting with guys would be on a girls night out agenda, but I really wanted to spend time with the girls.

"I don't know. I'm here with the girls," I protested, but Bernie almost pushed me out of my chair with "Go ahead. You love to dance!" Lynn added, "We're fine. Go. Go." And Betty added, "You never say no to a dance," as she whispered to the girls, "Guy magnet!"

As we're dancing, Jimmy says, "You dance well."

"Thank you. My name is Sam."

"Do you girls come here a lot?"

"Not really. This is a special occasion. We haven't seen Betty in almost a year and Lynn's birthday was last week. She's 18 and drinking is legal in New York so here we are."

"Well," says Jimmy. "I'm not going to keep you from your girls, but did you notice that guy over there at the table in the corner?"

I looked over. "Yeah."

"He would really like to meet you."

"So, why didn't he come over and ask me to dance?"

"Because he's a dunderhead."

I stopped dancing and looked over at the corner table again. "I'll introduce you if you want. He's really a nice guy, just a little on the shy side."

"Are you serious?"

"Yeah. I mean he really is a cool guy. He said you were cute."

Shaking my head and heading back to the table, I could only muster, "I, I don't know. This is pretty bizarre."

Bernie was the first to pick up the cue. "What's wrong Sunshine. Is he bothering you?"

"He wants me to meet his friend."

Jimmy interjected, "Chad, the one with the short dusty hair and five o'clock shadow over there in the corner."

"And you have reservations?" queried Bernie, her eyes almost popping out of her head.

"Yeah, are you nuts? He's gorgeous! I'll meet him," offered Betty.

Lynn added, "Don't let us stop you."

Jimmy shifted his pleading to the girls. "I would be more than happy to keep you girls company."

"Works for me!" said Bernie.

"Me too," added Betty.

"We're here to have some fun. Go ahead. Have some fun!" beamed Lynn.

"I just … I … I don't know. This is pretty strange," was all I could muster.

The girls gave me that "go ahead" look. Jimmy raised his hand as if to say "well".

"Okay, I guess. I'll give him ten minutes."

"Great," shouts Jimmy. "Yeah. If you introduce me to the girls, I'll introduce you to Chad."

So, I introduced Jimmy to my crew, picked up my drink and purse and the two of us headed to the corner table. Jimmy started to introduce me, but as my eyes locked on the lone occupant at the table, he just dismissively waved and headed back to the girls.

The guy at the table stood up – he was taller than I envisioned – and shook my hand. "Hi, I'm Chad and you're the most beautiful girl I've seen in here tonight."

"Sam," was all I could mutter. "Samantha. Samantha Casey but they call me Sam."

"It's a pleasure meeting you Samantha.

"Sam."

"Chadwick Watt. They call me Chad."

The waitress appeared, "Can I get you guys a refill?"

I responded, "I'll have what he's having," with Chad noting "It's just a regular old Coke. I have driving duties."

Blushing with a small smile on my face and a wink from the waitress, I said, "That's fine. So am I. So am I."

Chad started our conversation. "So, Samantha, what's your story."

I interrupted him. "Sam. Just Sam. Nobody calls me Samantha unless I'm in trouble."

"But it's such a beautiful name. It goes with your beautiful face. And I don't believe you could ever get in trouble," bringing color to my cheeks.

"You don't know me!"

He pressed, "I want to change that."

I immediately went on defense. "So, if I'm so beautiful why didn't you ask me to dance? You needed Cyrano?"

Chad put on what would become one of his patented smiles. "Are you saying Jimmy has a big nose?" bringing out another smile on my face along with a shake of my head. He continued, "Seriously, I don't do the flirt thing very well."

"Maybe not," I answered, "but you do have a way with words and you're pretty easy to look at."

It was Chad's turn to take control of this conversation again. "Okay. Okay. Let's start this over. My name is Chad and I still think you are most beautiful girl here.

"Sam. Just Sam. Thank you Mr. Watt. So what's your deal?"

"I don't have a deal," he said, "just enjoying some down time after classes. What about you? I'm sure you have a ..." He paused before continuing, "pretty interesting story to tell."

"You just don't know me ..."

"But I want to."

"Okay, what do you want to know?"

"Anything and everything. Are you from around here? Are you in school?"

"Well, I'm from New Jersey. I tell everybody Paterson, but it's really Totowa. And I do go to school at St. Vincent's over in The Bronx."

"Wow. We're practically neighbors. I go to Manhattan and live, well, lived in East Paterson. I have an apartment off campus with Jimmy and two other guys."

"Really. We **are** practically neighbors," I responded, not believing we lived so close to each other and go to school in the same neighborhood, but never ran into each other before. I don't know why I thought that. I mean, there are only about ten million people in the greater New York/New Jersey area and Totowa and East Paterson are separated by a very large Paterson.

"Go on. What year are you in at St. Vincent's?"

"Just finished my freshman year."

"Did it go well?"

"Well ..." stopping for a pregnant pause, "define well. I passed, but it was a struggle."

"I don't believe it!" said Chad feigning shock. "You look like a smart girl."

"I am a smart girl. Or, at least I was."

"Was?"

"I sailed through elementary and high school. In fact, I graduated in the top five of my class at Mary Help of Christians Academy. I always thought it was quite an accomplishment, but Mom always added, 'Of course, there were only 66 graduates.'"

"Still sounds pretty smart to me."

"Yeah, well, I think I was in the bottom five this year."

"What! Why?"

"I don't know. Maybe I had it too easy in high school. I didn't really have to study much. I was pretty intuitive on quizzes and I could write essays well. But in college, I had to actually work."

"Oh, come on," offered Chad. "It couldn't have been that bad."

"It was pretty bad. Between the commute, the challenges of college, the large classes and my new-found freedom, I saw unrecognizable grades so, as a vibrant 18-year-old, I did the natural thing ... party! Of course, my lifestyle choice did not sit well with Mom, but I was comfortable getting by in class and enjoying life on weekends."

"Aah. The party girl," mused Chad.

"Yeah. The party girl."

I didn't believe what I shared next, especially without the benefit of any rum. "It all came to a head one Saturday night in February. I returned home from a date around midnight only to be greeted by Mom. She informed me I had not one, but two calls from two different boys while I was 'out doing only God knows what with a third.' I actually was pretty proud of my popularity until she blurted out. 'What are my friends going to think? I'm raising the town tramp!'"

"Ouch!" said Chad.

"Yeah, that stung, although I'm still not sure whether it was because she suddenly categorized herself as a victim or the hurtful words. Anyway, verbal sparring and volume escalated from there with both of us saying way more than we should have. Dad even had to come in and send us back to our corners while he tried to sort out the mess. Poor dad. He had to listen to Mom's ranting, then he had to confront me. Both of us were crying. 'Dad, she had no right to say that,' I sobbed. 'I've never done anything wrong.' "

"Are things better now? Between you and your Mom? It's been, what, four months?"

"Well, we're not yelling at each other, but we're not really going out of our way to talk to each other either."

Chad tried to redirect the conversation; I think sensing how much my relationship with Mom bothered me. "Sounds like you have a pretty good relationship with your Dad though."

I could feel my mood lighten up. "I do. Daddy is the light of my life, my biggest fan and supporter. And I am his little girl."

"Let me guess. When you graduated, he bought you a new car … a Mustang … a convertible … gold … no, no, no, fire engine red."

With my mouth wide open, I cried out, "How did you know?"

Chad nodded toward the window and the parking lot.

"You cheated!" I exclaimed, taking a playful punch at Chad's arm while I started laughing and Chad smiled. "You cheated!"

"I watched you get out of the car. Couldn't resist, sorry. Go on, tell me more. What about your Mom?"

"Mom and I always had a different relationship. Even as a young girl there was a tension between us. I guess I always sought her approval, but Mom was so critical. I could get all A's and B's and Mom would focus on my lone C. I could get all dressed up and she would tell me my dress was wrinkled. She didn't like my friends or my music and always dismissed my opinions. To top it off, whatever happened, the whole town knew. Mom likes to **share** at the beauty parlor, the grocery store, at church, everywhere, although her version of events don't always mirror reality."

Chad seemed to be riveted to every word. "Do you have any good memories of your mom?"

"Well, yeah. Mom is a great cook. She can make anything taste good," I responded. "She isn't an accomplished chef or anything, but learned her kitchen skills from her mom, who had learned it from her mom. She always tells me recipes are guidelines and Mom always knew when to add a pinch of this, cut back on that or add or replace a missing ingredient. And she included me in the kitchen, firmly teaching me the basics from early on and sharing her skills as I grew up."

I stopped momentarily, then continued, "I remember one time when I was around five. I had always followed Mom around the kitchen and had already become aware of her critical nature. That morning, though, she handed me an apron and had me help mix the chocolate chips into the cookie dough. At five years old, that was a monumental task and a good part of the batter ended up on my once-clean apron. I started to cry, but Mom scooped me up in her arms and said, 'Sam, that's okay. That's why we wear aprons when we cook.' Yes, when it comes to the kitchen and its skills, Mom is open and forgiving. Just not the rest of the time."

"What about you?" asked Chad.

"What about me?"

"What do you like to do? What are your passions? What are you studying in school?"

The question caught me off guard. "I don't know. Let me think. Having good friends is important. That's why we came here tonight," I said, pointing to the rowdy table by the dance floor. "They're my best friends. We've been together since grade school, Bernie – actually Mary Bernadette but we call her Bernie – Betty and Lynn. We've been friends forever. They were always at the house, especially when Mom went on a cooking spree. They went to Mary Help of Christians with me. We had another friend who joined us on the weekends, Pat. She was the rebel and went to public school. Mom always picked on her, too."

"Friends. They're important," said Chad, hanging on every word.

"The Fearsome Foursome. That's what we call ourselves. But we headed off in different directions. Bernie went to cosmetology school and now works in a salon. Betty is at Fairleigh Dickinson while Lynn headed to the sunshine at the University of Miami.

After graduation, Pat moved to Rochester. Even though we were working part time last summer, whenever we had the chance, it was off to the Jersey Shore in our bikinis and cut off jeans. It was a staple of the summer, boy watching on the boardwalk at Seaside Heights and coyly teasing them."

Chad interjected, "And you did that well, I'm sure."

"Well, yeah!"

"Where did you work?"

"At the bakery in town. I still do part time."

"This is fascinating," said Chad. "Besides the shore, what else do you do for fun?"

A big smile beamed across my face as I pointed to the parking lot. "Since I got those keys in my hands, I am never home. It's off with my girls, often ending up at Falls View for two dogs, Frenchies well done and a large birch beer. And of course, we flirt with the guys too."

"There's that flirt word again," interjected Chad.

"There's nothing wrong with flirting."

"I didn't say there was. Just noting you said it again."

I was sort of embarrassed. "You must think I'm terrible."

"No. No. I think you're refreshing."

"That's a description I've never heard," drawing a smile from both of us.

I continued, "Sure, I like to party and toy with guys. Never gave them my real phone number though. I'm not into pick-ups or pick-up lines. I am, admittedly, a flirt …"

"That word again."

"Smarty, yes, I do enjoy leading guys on. But my upbringing and especially my four years with the nuns at Mary Help of Christians, you know, none of this and none of that, made me an in-control woman who knows when to put the brakes on in a relationship. A few guys never came back, but that's okay. If a guy isn't interested in more than my body – **my** body – and isn't willing to give me his heart, soul and undivided attention, then good riddance."

Chad clapped his hands. "That's my girl. Good for you!"

I was on a roll. I could sense I had him on the hook.

"A couple of months ago – don't tell anybody – I sat with Bernie for days on end when she thought she was pregnant. Her boyfriend skipped out as soon as the prospect of fatherhood was broached so it was up to me to hold her hand, hug her, comfort her, wipe her tears. 'What did I do?' 'What am I going to do?' 'Why did I listen to him when he told me he loved me?' It turned out to be a false alarm, but the experience steeled my will to stay in control of my life."

"I knew you were a closet softy. You have a special heart," he said softly.

"What about school?"

"There you go again, bringing up school!" I said as I crinkled the corner of my mouth. "Okay. I could have gone just about anywhere and was accepted at a number of major colleges. I chose St. Vincent's and its nursing program, although the sight of blood makes me sick. It was a case of trying to please everyone else but myself."

"Why? You know if you're not happy with yourself, it becomes awfully hard to find happiness."

The girls interrupted our conversation and asked me to go to the ladies room with them. Chad stood as I got up.

"Excuse me, sir. I'll be right back."

In the bathroom, the girls fixed their makeup, then started peppering me with questions.

Bernie started with, "Do we have to rescue you?"

"No, it's actually going well. He's rather quite charming. He's been open and appears to be honest. He hasn't talked much about himself but wants to know about me. And he listens. I know because he would occasionally bring up something I mentioned earlier in our conversation."

"You're so lucky," said Lynn.

"Lucky?" chimed in Bernie. "She was born with that talent."

"How about you guys?" I asked. "Do I have to rescue you?"

The girls looked at each other with Bernie answering for them, "We're doing fine!" Betty said, "I think Bernie's following your lead with Jimmy." And Lynn added, "He's kept us laughing and dancing …" with Betty confessing, "and drinking."

We decided to return to our tables. As I got to Chad's table, Chad stood up and held my chair.

"Miss me?" I asked as he pushed my chair back in.

"Yes I did. I wasn't sure if you would come back. I'm glad you did."

"Me too. Where were we?"

"I was scolding you about happiness."

"Oh yeah. You're right. I have to stop worrying about what others think and pay attention to my feelings."

"Let's see. To recap, we know you're a flirt …"

"Hey!"

"… with a big heart, inquisitive mind, beautiful face and ... gorgeous, soft hair," he said as he reached over and moved a strand of hair from my face. I could feel myself blush.

"What about you?" I asked, "I've been doing most of the talking."

Chad thought for a moment, pursing his lips. "Well, not much to tell. I'll be a senior at Manhattan next year. I'm an engineering major and an ROTC candidate …"

"ROTC?"

"Reserved Officers Training Corps. Air Force. When I graduate, I'll go into active service as a commissioned second lieutenant. My counselor and recruiter both think there's a good chance I could be assigned as a developmental engineer after basic training."

"Wow. You have your life planned out," I responded. "What does a developmental engineer do?"

"The short answer is I hope to use my engineering background to help design, develop, test or modify projects for the Air Force."

"That's pretty impressive. You must be a pretty smart guy."

"I don't know if I'm smart," said Chad, "but I take it seriously. I've worked hard. I didn't go to a lot of parties in college. Okay I did when I was a freshman too, but when I started to focus on the rest of my life I started taking it more seriously."

"Good for you," I said clapping my hands. "So you're not a flirt?"

"I didn't say that!" said Chad. "Let's say I'm more interested in knowing **who** I'm dating rather than just dating."

"So you **do** date."

"Yes I do. But I have to really like the real girl and with my schedule it's hard to find the time to find that real girl. I do like the Jersey Shore, Seaside Heights particularly. I don't flirt but I do girl watch. And no trip to the shore would be without a …"

"A sausage and pepper sandwich topped off with a Kohr's custard."

"You got it! Sausage and peppers with a Kohr's nightcap."

"I love the shore," I said as Chad again reached over and moved a wayward strand of hair from my face. "The sights. The sounds. The beach. The gentle roll of the waves. The cool breeze. The boardwalk. Skee Ball. The carousel."

"You hit a home run right there. There is nothing like Seaside Heights on a warm summer day and night."

"You're preaching to the choir, brother."

"Amen, sister."

Keeping the conversation going, I asked, "What about your family?"

"Pretty ordinary," Chad answered." Dad's an engineer ..."

"He drives trains?" I interrupted as I broke into a laugh.

"No. He's a structural engineer. He designs different components in buildings. Mom works part time when needed at a florist shop. And I have a younger brother Mike who will be a junior at East Paterson. Oh, and I have a dog, Jet. A mutt, really, but I've had him for years. I used to have goldfish, but they kept dying on me. All pretty ordinary."

During breaks between band sets, Mother's piped in music. As *When a Man Loves a Woman* wafted through the speakers, it signaled my cue. "Do you want to dance?"

"I'm not much of a dancer."

But I insisted as I took his hand and led him to the dance floor where Bernie and Jimmy were dancing.

"Come on. They can't be the only ones dancing."

"I'm warning you. Your toes are in danger."

"I'm not worried. So what if you step on a few toes. I have ten. Besides, this is nice and slow."

We started to dance. I put my head on Chad's shoulder. "You're doing great!"

"You make it easy."

As the song ended, I gave Chad a peck on the cheek. "Thank you."

"No. Thank you!"

We walked back to the table. On the way, I stopped and asked, "Does that make this our song?" to which Chad replied, "I hope so."

After we sat down and I took another sip of my Coke, I noticed the girls were getting a little loud. "I probably should take them home."

I also spotted the clock. "Wow, we've been talking for almost four hours."

"Time flies when you're having fun."

"Yeah, this was fun."

"I'll walk you to your car, if that's okay."

"I'd like that."

After collecting the girls, Chad and I walked to the car holding hands.

"This was fun," said Chad. "I'm so glad I got a chance to meet you."

"Even if you needed Cyrano to introduce me?"

Chad brushed back my hair and gave me a peck on the cheek. Then he whispered, "Can I call you sometime?"

"Sure. I would like that."

I reached into the car to get a piece of paper. The girls were now giggling. Bernie handed me a slip of paper with my phone number on it and I dutifully handed it to Chad.

"This isn't one of those fake numbers, is it?" he joked.

I looked at the paper. "Nope. That's my number," triggering a long good night kiss while girls not so subtly giggled.

"Sorry I bailed on you girls tonight," I said on the ride home. "I know this was supposed to be our night together."

"What?" was their response. "Really, it was just like the old days. Besides, we had fun. Jimmy certainly entertained us!"

As the tone got more serious, they commented, "He sure was cute." "Is he someone special?" "You going to see him again?" Yes, he was and I don't know and I don't know. "Ball is in his court," I assured each of them as I dropped them off. "He has my number. We'll see."

Chapter Four

Bernie popped in early Saturday morning and the two of us were getting ready to go downtown. The phone in kitchen rang. Mom answered and from the kitchen, yelled out, "Samantha! Phone!"

I walked into the kitchen and Mom handed me the phone. "Who is it?" I asked.

"I don't know! Another guy. What else is new," she tersely replied.

"Mom!" I snapped back as I grabbed the phone from her hand.

"Hello." I could hear an audible laugh through the receiver. "Chad?"

"Yeah, it's me," he said, still laughing.

"I'm so sorry about that. I told you Mom just blurts out whatever is on her mind."

"That's fine. Really. I just wanted to call and tell you I really enjoyed talking with you last night."

"It was fun. You were easy to talk to." I responded.

As Bernie walked into the kitchen, Chad asked "What are you doing?"

"Bernie and I were just getting ready to go downtown. You have any plans for the day?"

"Not for the day," he said, "but I was wondering what you were doing tonight?

"Tonight?"

Bernie realized who I was talking to. She started mouthing "Chad" and going into a pantomime faint or mouthing "I love you" or hugging herself in a mock embrace.

"Nothing," I answered.

"I'll plan something if that's okay. I really would love to see you again. Pick you up about six? We'll grab a bite to eat."

I found myself twirling my hair as I tried to hush Bernie.

"Well, sure. Where are we going?"

"I have something in mind. See you around six."

"Wait, what should I wear? Casual? Dressy?"

"You would look great in rags. Just dress comfortably. Nothing special. Gotta go."

"Okay. See you at six."

As I was hanging up the phone, Bernie blurted out, "Aw, you like him, don't you?" She started dancing around the kitchen. "Sammy's got a boyfriend. Sammy's got a boyfriend."

"Stop. I do not," I insisted as I felt my face start to flush.

In a panic I reached out to Bernie. "What should I wear? Let's go. I'll pick up a new outfit downtown."

Of course, a first date can't be kept a secret, so Betty and Lynn showed up to join Bernie in getting me "ready". At 6 p.m. on the dot, the doorbell rang, prompting Bernie to run out of room. She didn't quite make it before Mom opened the door.

"Good evening Mrs. Casey. I'm Chad."

Matter-of-factly she said, "You must be here for Sam. Come in. Everybody else is." Bernie intervened, "She's just about ready."

As I entered the living room, Chad simply stated, "Wow, you look beautiful." Then he turned to Mom and added, "I see where Sam gets her beauty."

Not wanting this dialogue to continue too much longer, I pushed Chad out the door as I said, "We won't be too late. See you later Mom."

I really didn't know what to expect but was pleasantly surprised as we walked to his car arm in arm and Chad opened the door for me. During the drive, he kept complimenting my outfit, camel-colored pants with stirrups and a bright, bold large check flannel shirt. I was likewise surprised as he pulled into the driveway at Falls View, pointed at me to wait and rushed around the car to open the door again.

He sidled up to the counter and said, "Two orders of two dogs all the way, Frenchies well done and two large birch beers." He turned to me and winked. "Right?"

All I could do was break into a big grin. *He remembered,* I thought. They were the best hot dogs I ever had!

After dinner, Chad drove to a parking lot next to a big white building with a bowed roof. "We're here."

Bewildered since I had never seen this place, I asked, "Where?"

"At Bowl-O-Mat. Ready for some fun?"

"Uh," I stammered. "I've never bowled before."

"What? Well, we're going to change that. You'll be able to cross it off your list of things to do in your life."

"But I don't know how to bowl."

"Well, we're going to change that," he repeated.

Chad got out of the car. I started to open the door, but Chad again put up his hand as he walked around the car to open the door.

"Milady," he said as he helped me out of the car.

"You know, I'm going to embarrass myself and you."

"Oh you are not. Besides, if you can get me to dance, I can get you to bowl."

We got inside the brightly lit bowling alley and the first thing Chad said was, "What size shoe do you wear?"

"What?"

"What size shoe do you wear?"

"Why?"

"Because we have to get you shoes."

"Why do I need shoes?" I asked as I lifted my foot. "I have shoes on."

"You need special shoes," he answered. "Those are pretty, by the way," referring to the new low heel Mary Jane flats I bought earlier.

"Thank you, I think. I wear a size five."

Chad turned to the counter person. "A size six for my girl and I'll take a 10."

I interjected, "No, it's a five."

"Trust me," said Chad. "You want it a little bigger. A size six."

We got the two-tone shoes and Chad started tying my shoelaces. "How's that? Feel good?"

"Pretty sexy. Bold use of colors," I responded as I twirled my feet in mini circles.

"Okay, now we'll get you a ball," Chad said as we headed toward racks filled with bowling balls. He mused, "Too heavy … Span is too small ... Ah, this one should work," as he handed me the blue-specked ball. "How's that?" I almost dropped the ball.

"Okay, now what am I supposed to do?" I asked.

Laughing, Chad responded, "Put your fingers in the holes. Good. Now drop the ball to your side."

I completely lost control of the ball as it bounced to the ground with a thud. Both of us broke into laughter, me out of embarrassment. "We'll get there," Chad assured me.

"Squeeze your fingers," he said. "Good. Now swing it a couple of times, not hard but gently."

After a few swings with the ball remaining in my grasp, we headed for our lane. In a reassuring tone, Chad says, "Now this is the easy part. You just roll the ball down the alley and knock down the pins."

"Easy, huh. Okay, I'll give it a try," but Chad stopped me. "Wait a minute. There's a form to it." He put his arms around me from behind and gently swung the ball with me. "Now, hold the ball by your chest. Take three steps while you're swinging the ball and release it."

I looked at Chad with a petrified smile on my face. "Got it."

I took three steps, swinging the ball as instructed, but it didn't release at the right point and lobbed onto the alley with a deafening crash.

"Ahhhh!" I gasped, but Chad ran up to me with an encouraging, "It's okay." He looked around and assured those in the adjacent lanes, "It's okay. First time bowling."

"I'm so embarrassed!" I squawked with my hands covering my eyes.

Chad was laughing – a good laugh – "Okay, the form wasn't exactly great, but look."

I peeked through my fingers as he proudly pointed out, "You knocked down a pin!"

We bowled – or I attempted to bowl – three games. My last game was a 26.

"That's not bad for your first time out," said Chad as he turned to the couple on the next lane. "Can you autograph this for her?"

The wife smiled, as the husband said, "Sure! It was an adventure bowling next to you guys. Good luck." He signed the score sheet and then handed the pen to his wife so she could sign too.

I could just muster, "I'm sorry. He made me come."

The woman said, "Don't be sorry. You two will be okay. It was fun watching him teach you." She gave her husband a longing look as they shook our hands. They then left hand-in-hand.

As we walked back to the car we recapped my first experience in a bowling alley, continuing as Chad pulled out of the parking lot. It took a couple of minutes for me to realize we were heading toward Garret Mountain. Chad parked in an area overlooking the city affectionately known as Lover's Cove; it was a place I had been to before a number of times. *This is it*, I thought. *Let the real Chad show up.*

Instead, when we got there, Chad got out of the car, went to the trunk, pulled out a blanket and placed it on the hood of his car. He opened my door, took my hand, led me to the blanket and helped me up. As I settled in with my back pressing on the windshield, he jumped up next to me.

"Boy, I really embarrassed you at the bowling alley," I said.

"Not me. I had fun," he responded.

"Well I embarrassed myself. How can something so simple be so hard?"

"Like anything else, it takes practice."

I offered, "You looked pretty comfortable."

"Well, I've been bowling for a long time ... junior leagues, high school leagues, night leagues. But I was rusty. I hadn't bowled in a couple of years."

"Wow. That's a lot of bowling."

"Yeah, I was captain of my high school team."

"I'm impressed," I said. "Is there anything you can't do?"

"There's a lot of things I can't do. But I always at least try."

"I've known you now for what, about 24 hours, but I feel I've known you forever," I said looking deeply into his brown eyes, sparkling in the moonlight with green flecks.

"I know. I feel the same way. It's like we were meant to meet. I can't explain it, but you know more about me than any of the other girls I dated. I feel so ..." He paused, then continued, "... comfortable with you. That's the word, comfortable. I've never felt that way before."

"That's a good word, comfortable," I responded softly. "I don't ever think I shared as much information with anyone else as I have with you, especially with someone I just met. And I say that from the bottom of my heart, not as the town flirt."

"You can flirt with me anytime," he answered as we melted into each other's arms ending in a satisfying kiss.

As we sat there cuddling, my head safely nestled on his chest just below his shoulder, Chad pointed toward the horizon. "What do you see?"

I thought for a moment. "Twinkling stars and twinkling lights. What do you see?"

"So much more. I see the past ..." he said. "... and the present ... and the future."

"That's pretty deep, Mr. Watt."

Chad continued, "See down there," as he pointed toward downtown. "That's our past. There's the Great Falls and downtown. We've both walked down those streets to Quackenbush's or Meyer Brothers. We probably caught the bus behind City Hall. Right in front of us is St. John's Cathedral. Can't miss it."

I squinted a little.

"Yeah, and I see St. Anthony's School. At least I think it's St. Anthony's. That's where I went to grade school. After we moved, I would take the bus from Totowa to downtown and walk to school from there."

Surprised, Chad asked, "Alone?"

"Yeah. It was a little scary the first few times, but the people on Beech Street got to know me and watched me. The ladies would come out and give me cookies and we would talk about school. If I missed a day or, God forbid, two, they would check up on me. Sister Mary would say, 'Samantha, Mrs. Donatelli called to make sure you were okay' or 'Mrs. Calabrese said she hadn't seen you in a few days.' She would always add, 'Do you make it a habit to talk to strangers, Samantha?' I usually walked with some of my friends to my grandma's house on East 22nd Street after school and Dad would pick me up there."

Shaking his head, Chad blurted out, "Nobody can ever accuse you of being an introvert."

"I have my quiet side."

"I'm sure you do. We all do. I was always the quiet one. I didn't have a lot of friends, just a few close ones."

Playfully I added, "I noticed. You needed Cyrano to introduce me to you."

"You're not going to let me forget that, are you?" He smiled as I shook my head back and forth.

He intuitively changed the subject, though. "Now look over there," he said, pointing directly below. "That's our neighborhoods today. Look, somebody just got pulled over."

I laughed then asked, "And the future?"

Chad swept his hand and pointed to the horizon. "That's our future. The world is our future. We can see and do it all. That's Route 80. It takes us anywhere we want to go."

I interjected, "You can even see New York City from here," with a shiver causing Chad to cover me with another blanket that lead to more cuddles and kisses.

I asked Chad, "What's your future?"

"I hope it's spending more time with you."

"Awe. I want to spend more time with you, too"

More seriously, Chad added, "I'm pretty focused on my career, both engineering and the Air Force. And I take my studies seriously. What about you?"

"Haven't thought much about it, to be honest."

He pressed me. "What would you like do? I mean, we both know you don't like the sight of blood."

"Just don't know. I better get serious about school, though, huh?"

"I'll help you," said Chad. "No, I want to help you."

"You say that now. Let's talk in September."

We spent the rest of the evening just talking and cuddling with an occasional kiss, all the time oblivious to the steamy windows of the cars around us. I didn't want it to end.

The night ended, but our relationship didn't. Instead, it continued to grow throughout that summer. Chad and I spent a lot of time together and got to know each other better, and he never wore off. He saw me at my worst when I had a summer cold, but still said I was beautiful. He put up with my moods, gently turning my sour side into a sweeter one with just the right phrase or joke. He encouraged and challenged me every time we went out.

And we went out a lot. We went to the shore where we played in the sand and surf, played Skee Ball and ate our signature sausage and peppers sandwiches followed by a Kohr's frozen custard. We went bowling – I did get a little better – and to the drive-in. We had picnics on Garret Mountain. We went on long drives to High Point and the western New Jersey countryside.

Chapter Five

By summer's end, I was smitten with him, and it appeared to be mutual. After all, for most of the summer, where he was, I was.

We learned a lot about each other but still knew our boundaries. Sure, there was plenty of holding hands, hugging, kissing, and even a little fondling, but we both knew when to slow down. I think that's what I loved about him – yes, I said "loved." He listened patiently to my words and my heart. He gave me his prime time, not the leftovers. He praised me. He surprised me. He courted me. He treated me like a queen in front of other people. And he never, ever pressured me.

I wasn't sure where our relationship would go when school started again. It changed, but not all that much. Even though we went to school near each other in The Bronx, we lived in different states, so phone calls were expensive. Yet he found a way to keep in touch. He would call just to say, "I love you!" or "I miss you!" He always planned either a Friday or Saturday night date, usually in the city. We went on weekday walks through Riverside Park or VanCortland Park. We had study dates at the library or his place – and he forced me to study! We went to ball games, museums and plays in the city. And it wasn't unusual for me to receive an unexpected card in the mail that simply said, "I was thinking about you."

Mom recognized the change, too, and invited the Watts over for Thanksgiving.

"Thank you so much for inviting us over," said Mrs. Watt. "I wish I could have done more."

"No bother. I do this every year, don't I Joe?"

"She's just a cookin' fool," Dad said, patting his tummy. "Can't you tell? And Sam helped too, didn't you honey?"

"Yes, Dad," I responded.

"Sam's pretty good in the kitchen. I taught her well," offered Mom.

Dinner went well, although Mom managed to embarrass me over and over with her questions and her revelations about my childhood. "Samantha was a cute baby. Do you want to see some pictures?"

"Of course!" said Mrs. Watt. "I have some of Chad in my wallet."

Mom continued, "Sam was pretty shy and quiet as a child. She grew out of that." After a pause, she added, "She was book smart but didn't have much common sense."

Chad quickly picked up on the cue. Looking at me he said, "We have to go. We're meeting Jimmy and Bernie, remember Sam?"

"Yeah. Yeah. We told them we would meet them."

"Mrs. Casey, great dinner. Mr. Casey, thank you for having us over. Mom, Dad, I'll see you later."

When we got to the car, I exhaled. "Thanks for rescuing me!"

"No problem. You would have done the same for me."

In the middle of traffic Chad suddenly pulled the car over and took my hand. "You know I love you, Sam. Every day I love you more. But I have to know if you feel the same way."

I was stunned. I never expected those words at this time. "Yes! Yes! Without a doubt!" And there on the side of the road I grabbed his head in my hand and planted a long, deep kiss on his lips. At that moment we officially became a couple.

Not much changed as went through the rest of the school year. We still had to get through his stint with the Air Force, and I still had two more years of school, so we never talked about the future or marriage. In fact, we never talked about getting engaged either. Still, he would indulge my fantasies when we walked past a jewelry store or bridal shop, always with a big grin on his face. We went to a play and walked the streets of New York City during the Christmas season. I stayed at his apartment a couple of times during the winter when the weather got bad, sleeping in his bed … alone. He wouldn't have it any other way. By February, I started keeping some clothes at his place so I could get ready "properly" if we went into the city.

Mom, of course, was not happy with my new arrangements. I know she was only trying to protect me, but it hurt that she didn't trust me.

I remember the first time I called her to tell her I wasn't coming home that night because of a storm. Although I could only hear her rant, I could visualize her arms flailing as she paced back and forth as far as the phone cord would allow. During a pause in the tirade, I could hear her explaining to Dad – from her perspective – how his daughter insisted on being a floozy. As I eavesdropped on the conversation, it was "What will the neighbors say?" Dad, who apparently had just come home, tried to calm her down with, "It is pretty nasty out there."

Next thing I knew, Dad was on the phone. He wanted to know what was going on, then insisted on talking to Chad. I only heard one side of the conversation. "Yes, sir." "It is … very slippery." "No, no, sir. I'll be on the couch." "I will." "Good night, sir."

During spring break, I went with Chad and his family to Florida, and I was so proud to be his escort to a military ball just before his graduation. Tears of joy were in my eyes as he walked up to receive his degree.

Chapter Six

We only had a few weeks between graduation and his assignment at Wright-Patterson Air Force Base in Ohio. Two weekends before he had to leave, I decided to cook him dinner, even though I had never prepared an entire meal by myself.

As I was wrapping up dinner preparations, Chad arrived. The table was set and front door was open.

From the kitchen I heard him. "Hi hon." I met him steps from the door and escorted him into the dining room. "Right on time as usual." I gave him a quick kiss and told him to sit.

"Just the two of us? Where's your Mom and Dad?"

"Just the two of us. Mom and Dad went to visit Mom's cousin in Delaware for the weekend. I thought we could celebrate before you leave."

"Wow, that …" he paused and swept his hand over the table. "… this looks great and so do you."

"You say that to all your girls?" I laughed. "I'm still in my sauce-stained apron and have flour dusting my hair. I look real great," I said as I lit the candles. "I'll be right back. I just want to freshen up a bit."

"Take your time. Everything smells great."

I returned to the dining room, bringing the food to the table. "I hope you like it."

"I know it will be great. Smells so good. Besides, you made it."

"All by myself," I beamed. "Actually it's the first time I made an entire meal by myself. I'm a little nervous."

"Okay. What's on this special menu?"

"It's Chicken Chasseur with glazed carrots, Pommes Anna and French bread. And I picked up a nice Bordeaux."

"What's Chicken Chasseur?" he asked as he started to eat.

"It's baked chicken breast in a tarragon mushroom sauce."

"Ummm. This is good. I never saw potatoes like this. It's almost like a potato cake."

"It is. It's a pain in the neck to make but for you, it was worth it."

"You say the sweetest things," said Chad as he shoveled in another mouthful. "But you're the sweetest!"

"Speaking of sweet, I made a Pumpkin and Pecan Cheesecake for dessert."

We talked about dinner and his military service as we finished dinner.

"That was really, really good. I mean really, really good. Thank you," said Chad as he gave me a big kiss. "Let me help you clean up."

"No. Go sit down and make yourself comfortable. I'll just let the dishes soak."

Together we cleared off the table then went to the couch. I brought in the wine and laid my head on Chad's shoulder. We started kissing when all of a sudden I started unbuttoning Chad's shirt.

"Are you sure about this?" asked Chad.

"Definitely," I answered as I lead his hand to the buttons on my blouse. We kissed and started fondling. I got up and let my pleated Gracie swing skirt fall to the floor. I reached out to Chad and lead him to my bedroom.

"Are you sure about this?" Chad asked again.

"Definitely."

We made love and exploded in ecstasy. We laid in each other's arms for what seemed like hours before Chad eventually rolled over and dozed off. I just kept staring at him, my head resting on my hand.

But as the euphoria waned and the afterglow ebbed, second thoughts crept into my mind. I felt what we had done was right, but my upbringing nagged my thoughts. *What did I do? What am I going to do? Why did I listen to him when he told me he loved me? He's leaving next week. Is he going to leave me now? What did I do?* There I was, literally and figuratively stuck buck-naked between a wall and a naked man. How had an in-control woman lost so much control?

Chad woke up and rolled over, kissing my arm. He propped his head on his hand and kissed me.

"Are you okay?" he asked.

It took me a few seconds to answer with a smile, "Yes. I'm better than okay." Then I grabbed a blanket to hide my nakedness on my way to the bathroom. "I just have to pee." I threw in a towel for Chad.

When I returned, Chad was already getting dressed. *I knew it*, I thought to myself. He again asked, "Are you alright?"

"Yeah," I answered. "Why are you getting dressed?"

"I probably should be going. I don't want to give the neighbors anything to talk about."

I protested. "You don't have to go. Really!"

"I know. You do know I love you."

"Right. Do you have to go?" I pleaded.

"I probably should. This was …" he stammered. "This was an amazing night. Thank you so much."

"But I don't want you to go."

"I don't want to go either, but I should."

"Why?" I asked. Tears started to roll down my cheeks.

Chad took me in his arms. "Listen, I love you. But it's best I go."

"But …"

"Shh." He gave me a gentle kiss. "Just know I love you. I'll talk to you tomorrow."

Chapter Seven

As his taillights faded down the street, I convinced myself my actions had ruined a perfect relationship. I put on my long flannel nightgown, comfy robe and fuzzy slippers, made myself a cup of tea and wrapped myself in a blanket on the couch. The minute hand on the clock inched ever so slowly. Twelve after ... what felt like forever ... thirteen after ... another eternity ... fourteen after ... With each minute, another argument raged in my mind. *What we did was right. What we did was wrong. What did I do? What am I going to do? When will daylight come so I can call Bernie?* I needed her, and I needed her now.

Shortly after eight o'clock, I made the call. Bernie's mom answered and got her for me. She was still half asleep when she answered, but as soon as I said with a crackling voice, "Bern," she knew something was wrong and immediately became alert. "What's wrong, Sam? What's wrong?"

"Bern ..." I said through sobs.

"What's wrong, Sam? What's wrong?"

"I think I messed ..." Bernie cut me off. "I'll be there in a half hour."

Bernie found me crying, still curled up on the couch. I reached up to her. A sudden, new burst of tears started flowing. Bernie sat down and gave me a big hug. "Calm down, Sam. Tell me what happened."

"I cooked him a special dinner. It was just the two of us. We had a bottle of Bordeaux ..." I said.

"Go on. Nothing to cry about yet unless you burned the dinner or spilled the wine all over him."

"No. We started making out on the couch. And I got up …" I said, breaking into a new spasm of sobs. "… took my skirt off and led him to the bedroom …"

Bernie interrupted, "And …"

"We …" I had to stop before continuing. "… made love."

"Did it feel right?" asked Bernie as she continued to feed me the tissues.

"Yes … No …" I said shrugging my shoulders. "I don't know."

"Well, do you love him?"

"Yes, but that's the problem. I don't know if he still loves me."

With a quizzical look, Bernie asked, "What makes you say that? Did he say something?"

"No. He said he loved me …" I answered. I took a second to wipe my nose and eyes. "… but he went home."

Bernie's eyes widened. "Okay, you're thinking too hard. You guys have been going out for a year …"

I interrupted, "I know, but we never went all the way. He knew I wanted to wait, and I thought he wanted to wait. But we got caught up in the moment and one thing led to another …" – another tear wipe – "… and now I'm afraid he's gone."

"That's silly. I've seen you two together. He not only loves you, but he respects you too. That's more than a lot of guys …" I cut her off.

"But, that's the problem. I don't know if he will still respect me."

"Well, maybe you should talk to him. Come on, enough of this pity party. We can't change the past. You know that. Hell, you told me that, remember? But you still can control the future. You're the same fun-loving girl you were yesterday," she said. With a smile and a poke of my arm, she added, "Only today you're a woman."

Through puffed eyes and a wavering voice, I responded, "I think I liked it better when I was still a girl. Besides, we didn't even have dessert."

Bernie laughed. "I think you did."

She was right, of course, but I was positive Chad would soon be history. He was leaving for Ohio the following week, and I would quickly become a memory.

Chapter Eight

Later that day, the phone rang. "Hello?" I offered in a soft, reticent voice, knowing who it probably was. I was right. It was Chad.

"Are you okay?" he said. "I sensed something was wrong when I left last night. I didn't mean to hurt or upset you. Do you want to talk?"

All I could do was whisper, "No, everything is fine. Last night was …" I paused before continuing, "… well …" followed by another pause before adding, "… special. I'm okay, just a little tired. How about a rain check?"

Chad was taken aback, but said, "Okay, Sam, but remember, I love you!"

The next night, Chad called again. This time Mom answered the phone. "Hello. Chad? Just a minute, I'll get her."

Mom came to my bedroom but through the door I responded with "Tell him I'll call him later."

Completely in the dark, Mom delivered the message, "Chad, she said she will call you later." After some hesitation, she added, "Okay. I'll tell her. Bye."

The next night, Chad called again. Intuitively knowing who it was, I answered curtly, "Hello," followed by a just as curt, "Hi Chad."

"You didn't call me back last night," he chided.

"I'm sorry. I got wrapped up in a project and next thing I knew it was too late to call."

Chad wasn't buying the excuse. "Something else is wrong. I can hear it in your voice. Was it Saturday night? I mean Sam …"

I interrupted him and in an annoyed tone answered, "Nothing is wrong. I know you're busy and I got busy. This has nothing to do with Saturday."

But Chad still wasn't buying into the excuses. "I don't believe you," he said. "I think we should talk."

"Whatever," I tersely responded. "You're making a big deal out of nothing. Besides, in a couple of weeks you won't even be able to talk to me."

"What? Not talk to you? Why?"

"You'll be on the base and really busy. You just won't have time for me."

His voice turned stern. "Sam, you're not making any sense. How about if I pick you up and we'll get a Coke or something."

"Not tonight. But we'll get together before you leave. I have to go. Talk to you later," I said before he could respond and before my tears betrayed me. As I was hanging up the phone, I could hear him saying, "Sam? Sam?"

I knew we should talk about Saturday night, but I wasn't ready. And with each passing day, I started insulating my heart from breaking.

About15 minutes later, there was a knock at the front door. There was Chad. "What are you doing here?" I asked.

"Picking you up. We're going to the diner."

"I don't feel like going out," I said as Mom came into the room.

"Everything okay?" she asked, sensing something just wasn't right.

"Yeah," I said, "Chad just stopped to take me out for a Coke."

"That's right, Mrs. Casey. I haven't seen Sam in a few days and I needed to see her smile," which resulted in me giving him a funny look.

"Well, are we going?" I asked incredulously.

We headed to the diner in silence. After the waitress brought two Cokes to the table, Chad broke the ice. "Okay. What's this chill all about?"

"There's no chill …" I started to say, prompting Chad to blurt out, "Bullshit!"

That got my attention – along with others in the diner. I hadn't ever heard him say anything even remotely off-color.

Chad quieted down, reached across the table to hold my reluctant hands. "Something is wrong." He said, "Is this about Saturday?"

As my eyes misted, I said "No, nothing is wrong. How many times do I have say it. Everything is fine." I pulled my hands back. "Saturday," as I started taking a deep breath, "was …" – another deep breath – "… was …" – a third deep breath, more like a muffled sob – "wonderful. I guess you …" – another pause. "I guess I thought you should spend some time with your family since you're going to Ohio next week."

Bewildered, Chad answered, "I spend enough time with my family. I want to spend my time with you. But there is something else going on. I know you wanted to wait and I'm sorry we didn't. I wanted to wait, too. But it doesn't change anything. I love you, even more."

"I know and ..." I started to say but not without tears dripping from my eyes, "... it ..." was all I could get out before another deep breath was needed, "...was ..." followed by another sob, "... great. I'm not sorry we made love ..."

Chad interrupted me and wiped my tears. "Yes, we made love. We did not just have sex." He reached out and grabbed my hands again. "Sam, I love you."

"But you went home! You left me alone!" I cried.

Chad leaned back in his booth seat. "That's what this is about?"

The water works were in full blast. "I ..." gasping before catching enough breath. "... I guess so. I got scared you didn't love me anymore."

"Wow," said Chad. "I ... I didn't realize ..."

Through the tears I said, "I didn't want to lose you, but I felt you got what you wanted, and I was ... excess baggage."

"Excess baggage?" Chad responded. He reached across the table to again wipe my tears and push away the strands of hair from my face. "You're the best thing that ever happened to me. Truth is I was embarrassed. I knew you wanted to wait and so did I. But we didn't and I don't regret a minute."

"Me neither," I said. I tried to recompose myself.

"Wow. I wish you would have told me this on Sunday. I was afraid, too. I was afraid you lost respect for me and I didn't want to lose you Sam. I love you!"

With that, he reached into his pocket and pulled out a little box. I opened it. It was two white gold rings studded with small diamonds and soldered together with a big gap in the middle. I looked at Chad with a quizzical expression on my swollen face. "What's this?"

"That's the wedding ring I picked out for you," said Chad nonchalantly. He reached into his other pocket and pulled out another little box. I opened it. It was another white gold ring with a diamond proudly standing in a simple yet elegant setting. "That's the engagement ring I picked out for you."

He then put the two settings together. "A perfect fit. Just like you and me. They were made for each other. Just like you and me."

I was speechless.

"Samantha Marie Casey, will you marry me?"

The conversation at the table started to draw some attention. I was still speechless until Chad asked again, "Samantha Marie Casey, will you marry me?"

All I could say was "Are you sure?"

"I'm positive. Samantha Marie Casey, will you marry me?"

This time with the tears transformed to joy, I exclaimed, "Yes! … Yes!"

The other patrons started clapping, whistling and yelling "way to go" as I pushed my left hand out.

All of a sudden, the box lid snapped shut. "No …" said Chad, causing our fellow patrons to stop clapping. Some whispered "What did he say?" The waitress dropped her coffee pot.

But Chad continued, reopening the box lid. "… not sometime in the future. I mean right now, this weekend. Sam, I love you. I don't want to wait to make you my wife."

The diner, which just seconds ago was buzzing then went totally silent, started erupting again, especially when I responded, "I love you, too. This weekend it is!"

The claps turned into hugs and handshakes from total strangers. The couple in the booth next to ours picked up our check. Our waitress brought us a piece of cake she had cut into the shape of a heart. Even the cooks came into the dining area to offer their well wishes. There we were, two young lovers being treated like movie stars. Amid the commotion, we were isolated in our own little world, existing just for each other.

For the rest of the evening, we planned our wedding, eloping to Maryland. We promised not to tell anyone except Jimmy and Bernie since we wanted them in the wedding. Besides, Jimmy sort of knew what Chad was thinking and if Jim knew, Bernie knew. After all, they were a couple, too.

We agreed not to tell our parents or friends. We knew eloping would disappoint them, but this was our moment, and we didn't want any lectures.

It was a little surreal. Both of us were more, well, practical. Chad said he would make all the arrangements. He would pick me up early on Saturday morning and we would head to Maryland. All I needed to do was come up with a cover story; of course, spending the weekend with Bernie was perfect.

Chapter Nine

Even though it was late, as soon as I got home, I called Bernie. "You have some time tomorrow? We have to talk about something…"

Bernie cut me off. "He did it, didn't he? He asked you to marry him! That son of a gun. I knew it. I knew it!"

"Well, yeah. That's why we have to talk …"

"I'll be there in 30 minutes."

When Bernie got here, I told her all about the proposal.

"Wow. I'm impressed. Jimmy told me Chad was going to ask you to marry him, but we both thought it would be later this year. This weekend. Elope. I didn't see that coming with Chad!"

"Me neither. Not in my wildest imagination."

"Okay, said Bernie, "this is between us. We'll go shopping tomorrow." As she gave me the biggest hug ever and started to cry herself, she added, "You'll be the most beautiful bride ever. You'll be the most beautiful bride ever."

Friday, we headed downtown. After looking at what seemed like hundreds of dresses, I picked a long white A-line satin dress with a criss-cross chiffon bodice and a behind-the-neck tie at Quackenbush's. Bernie insisted I wear my hair up, and she found an orchid hairpiece that complemented the ensemble. Over at Meyer Brothers, we went into the lingerie department, where she picked out a short-style peignoir set as a gift to me. Both the gown and robe were embellished with embroidered lace and beads. The gown had chiffon flounces on the sleeves and hem, and a chiffon tie at the waist.

I spent Friday night at Bernie's house. Chad and Jimmy picked us up bright and early Saturday morning. As we entered the Garden State Parkway, I realized we were going through with this. We pulled into the parking lot at the Sutton Inn in Elkton, Maryland, around noon and checked in. Bernie and I went to one room and Jim and Chad went to the other so we could get ready.

By four, we were at the Historic Little Wedding Chapel. Chad looked dashing in his uniform. He kept staring at me in my dress. As he took my hand, he whispered in my ear, "You are so incredibly beautiful. I am so proud you agreed to be my wife." I whispered back, "I love you."

Dennis Kern, the justice of the peace, started the ceremony. "A good marriage must be built on the foundation of this commitment. In marriage the little things are the big things. It is never being too old to hold hands. It is remembering to say 'I love you' at least once a day. It is never going to sleep angry. It is standing together and facing the world. It is speaking words of appreciation and demonstrating gratitude in thoughtful ways. It is having the capacity to forgive and forget. It is giving each other an atmosphere in which each can grow. It is a common search for the good and the beautiful. It is not only marrying the right partner – it is being the right partner. Are you Samantha and Chadwick ready to embark on this journey?"

I answered, "I am." Chad chimed in, "Yes, all the way."

Justice Kern asked us to hold hands, then looking at me, continued, "Samantha, repeat after me, I, Samantha Marie Casey,"

"I, Samantha Marie Casey,"

"take you Chadwick William Watt,"

"take you Chadwick William Watt,"

"to be my husband, to have and to hold from this day forward;"

"to be my husband, to have and to hold from this day forward;"

"for better or for worse;"

"for better or for worse;"

"for richer, for poorer;"

"for richer, for poorer;"

"in sickness and in health;"

"in sickness and in health;

"to love and to cherish from this day forward until death do us part."

"to love and to cherish from this day forward until death do us part."

He then said, "Samantha, do you affirm these words as vows?" and I quietly but confidently answered, "I do."

Justice Kern then turned to Chad. "Chad, repeat after me, I, Chadwick William Watt,"

"I, Chadwick William Watt,"

"take you Samantha Marie Casey,"

"take you Samantha Marie Casey,"

"to be my wife, to have and to hold from this day forward;"

"to be my wife, to have and to hold from this day forward;"

"for better or for worse;"

"for better or for worse;"

"for richer, for poorer;"

"for richer, for poorer;"

"in sickness and in health;"

"in sickness and in health;"

"to love and to cherish from this day forward until death do us part."

"to love and to cherish from this day forward until death do us part."

He then asked, "Chadwick, do you affirm these words as vows?" Chad enthusiastically said, "I do."

Justice Kern explained we would now exchange rings to symbolize our commitment to each other. "Rings are derived from humble beginnings of imperfect metal to create something striking where there was once nothing at all. It is customarily worn on the ring finger as it is the only finger with a vein running directly to the heart. The wearing of the rings is a visible, outward sign the couple have committed themselves to one another."

He instructed Chad to take my left hand. "Chadwick, repeat these words. I give you this ring, as a symbol of our love,"

"I give you this ring, as a symbol of our love,"

"for today and tomorrow, and for all the days to come."

"for today and tomorrow, and for all the days to come."

"Wear it as a sign of what we have promised on this day"

"Wear it as a sign of what we have promised on this day"

"and know my love is present,"

"and know my love is present,"

"even when I am not."

"even when I am not."

With that, Chad slipped his specially designed ring on my finger.

Turning to me, Justice Kern instructed me to take Chad's left hand. "Samantha, repeat these words. I give you this ring, as a symbol of our love,"

"I give you this ring, as a symbol of our love,"

"for today and tomorrow, and for all the days to come."

"for today and tomorrow, and for all the days to come."

"Wear it as a sign of what we have promised on this day"

"Wear it as a sign of what we have promised on this day"

"and know my love is present,"

"and know my love is present,"

"even when I am not."

"even when I am not."

I slipped a newly purchased gold band on Chad's finger.

Justice Kern continued, "By sharing your vows and exchanging rings here today you both have decided to share the rest of your lives together. You are no longer two separate people but one couple together. We have a tradition here which symbolizes this unity through the pouring of these two individual containers of sand." He extended his hand toward two vials of sand. "One," he said, "represents you, Samantha, and all you were, all you are and all you will ever be, and the other represents you, Chadwick, and all you were and all you are and all you will ever be. As these two containers of sand are poured into the third container, the individual containers of sand will no longer exist, but will be joined together as one. Just as these grains of sand can never be separated and poured again into the individual containers, so will your marriage be united as one for all of your days."

We walked over to the adjoining table and in unison, poured our respective vials of sand into a larger vase.

As the last grains settled, Justice Kern took our hands and said, "Samantha and Chadwick you have professed your love by exchanging your vows. You have symbolized your commitment by exchanging rings. And you have expressed the end of your individual lives by the pouring of the unity sand. By the power vested in me I now pronounce you husband and wife. Chad you may kiss your bride."

And he did!

Justice Kern then looked at the small group of witnesses and proudly exclaimed, "It's my great honor and privilege to be the first to present to you Mr. and Mrs. Chadwick William Watt!"

Following the ceremony, Jimmy and Bernie joined us for dinner. We were thankful for all Bernie and Jim had done for us, and we predicted they would be next. It didn't happen. Jimmy was offered a job in Maine and, although they tried a long-distance relationship for a while, they drifted further and further apart. They remained friends through the years, although Jimmy eventually got married. Bernie never found Mr. Right.

We left them around eight and retired to our room, which the inn staff had cleaned and freshened with rose petals on the oversized bed. They also left a bottle of champagne chilling.

We talked, trying to figure out how we were going to tell our parents, about where we would live, and fantasizing about our future together. Around 10 p.m., I went into the bathroom and walked out in my negligee. It did not stay on long, and this time it felt right – very right.

Chapter Ten

Sunday afternoon, we made it back to my house. As I opened the door, I called out, "Mom? Dad?"

Mom came in from the kitchen, while Dad came downstairs from his attic workroom.

With a big smile I announced, "Mom. Daddy. Chad and I got married."

The smile quickly started to fade as Mom cried out, "You did what? When? Where? What were you two thinking?"

I started to answer, but could just get out, "M…"

"No! No!" she ranted, "This is wrong! This is wrong! Are you pregnant?"

Stunned, I answered, "No, Mom. I'm not pregnant and this isn't wrong!"

But she continued, "How could you do this to us?" and then looking at Chad with cold steel eyes, added, "How could you do this? How could you take advantage of my daughter?"

"Mom," I interjected. "This was our decision, not Chad's, ours."

But she continued, "And what am I supposed to tell everybody? My daughter got married and didn't care enough to tell me?"

"That's not fair," I countered. "Mom listen to yourself. Why do you always have to be the center of attention? Can't you be happy for us?"

But, shaking her head, she persisted, "No. This is a mistake you'll regret for the rest of your life. After all we've done for you. You're so ungrateful."

By now I was in tears. Mom just walked away with her hands waving and talking to herself. Dad came over and gave me a hug with tears in his eyes. "I'll talk to Mom. I'll make her understand. We went through this exact same thing. We eloped just before I was deployed during the war."

That news stunned me.

"Congratulations! I love you," said Dad. "Don't ever forget that!"

He turned to Chad with an outstretched hand that evolved into a hug. "Welcome to the family, as crazy as it is. You just better make sure you take care of my little girl."

"I will, sir," promised Chad.

"Have you told your folks yet?"

Chad replied, "No. We were going there next."

"Go. I'll take care of things here."

As we walked toward the car, I was dazed and confused. I knew Mom could be animated, but that comment about eloping really shook me. As we drove toward Chad's house, he tried to alternately calm me down and reassure me. "We have each other, right?" he said. And probably a half dozen times said, "Hey, Sam. I love you. No regrets."

I fixed my makeup and hair as best I could before going into Chad's house. He opened the door and called out, "Mom. Dad. I want to introduce you to my wife, Samantha Watt."

Chad's Mom started to cry but without the histrionics. She reached out to me and grabbed my hand. "Let me see that ring. That's beautiful," and with a big hug added, "Welcome."

She turned to Chad with a playful scowl and a punch in the arm. "And you! You could have warned me!"

Dad Watt enthusiastically said, "Congratulations, you two," as he gave me a hug and shook Chad's hand. "I never would have thought you would just run off."

As he put his arm around Chad's Mom, she gave him an admiring glace. "Do your parents know?" she asked.

"Yes," I responded, "but it didn't go so well. Mom wasn't very happy."

"It probably came as quite a shock to her. I know it surprised us. I knew Chad loved you, but to elope ..." she said catching her breath. "I never ever gave that a thought. But I'm happy for you two. You were made for each other. You complement each other."

Dad Watt chimed in. "Mom's right. We can't be any happier for you two. Why don't you get going and I'll give Joe a call. Maybe we can have dinner tomorrow night and celebrate."

Chad's brother Mike bounded down the stairs to investigate the noise. "What did I miss?"

His Mom answered, "Your brother got married."

"Whaaat?" exclaimed Mike. Looking at me and grabbing my hands, he said, "Sam, how did you get roped into this?"

Dad Watt gave that look, knowing how brothers act. "Mike!"

"No, seriously bro, congrats." He shook Chad's hand and reached over to me as he added, "Welcome to the family. How come I wasn't invited to the party?"

Dad Watt explained, "Because they eloped."

"Wow. Cool," said Mike, but Mom Watt put up her finger and quickly told him, "Don't get any ideas."

"Hey, you guys, seriously, congratulations," said Mike. "Finally, I get a sister, an older sister to protect me."

Both parents planned a dinner with us the next day. We agreed, but on our way back to the hotel, I told Chad we were being set up. "You know they want to separate us," I said.

"I know," said Chad, "but that's not going to happen."

Mom Watt started the conversation at dinner with, "So, were you as surprised as we were with the big news?"

Mom replied, "Surprised is an understatement! I guess we have to help them figure out what they're going to do next."

"Mom, we're right here," I interjected.

"Of course, dear. It's just there are a lot of things that have to be considered."

Mom Watt said, "Liz is right." And Dad Watt added, "Of course, we're not going to tell you what you have to do. I mean, you already made a pretty big decision on your own." My dad contributed, "Yeah. It was a pretty big decision."

Chad tried to divert the conversation. "We know and we're sorry if we disappoint ..." but his dad interrupted him. "You didn't disappoint us." Dad added a quick "No."

Dad Watt continued, "But you did catch us off guard."

Then it came.

Mom matter-of-factly said, "I think you should stay home while Chad figures out arrangements in Ohio." Dad also had a million reasons why his little girl should stay home.

I protested. "Then why did we even get married? I mean, we want to be together. That was the whole point."

"Yes, dear, but Chad's going to be pretty busy. Besides, you still have school. You're not going to throw away the last two years are you?"

"Of course not," I countered, tersely adding, "They **do** have schools in Ohio you know."

Mom Watt didn't help. "You're more than welcome to stay with us too." Dad Watt suggested converting the breezeway and garage into a nice little apartment.

Mom thanked him for the offer, but adamantly quipped, "That's a lot of work, Chad. Sam can stay at home in her room."

"Well, sure, but I thought she might want a little place of her own."

My turn. "I do. But I want it in Ohio with my husband."

Chad backed me up. "I'm with Sam on this one. I'm sure I'm not the first guy in the Air Force to get married."

But Mom, like a pit bull, wouldn't let it go. "Have either of you even looked at apartments? And after basic training, is Chad even going to stay in Ohio?"

Chad responded, "I'm pretty sure. Of course, there are no guarantees. I'll know more in six weeks after commissioned officer training in Alabama."

"See? Six weeks," said Mom waving her hands.

I simply said, "I don't know."

Mom quickly added, "And we have to get you married in the eyes of God."

Mom Watt agreed. "Oh, certainly. You need your marriage approved by the church."

I tried to interject our feelings. "We don't have …" but Mom looked at Chad's Mom and said, "We'll make the time, right Catherine?"

"Of course. We'll take care of everything, the church, the priest, the reception."

"We don't want anything big and …" I countered, but Mom, in her typical tone, asked, "Sam, don't you care about anyone else but yourself?"

Chad tried to defend me. "We're pretty content with what we did. If we wanted a big church wedding we would have planned it."

This time it was his Mom who squashed our thoughts. "Chad, you don't have to plan anything. Liz and I will tend to the details."

Feeling defeated, all I could muster was a "Whatever ..." while Chad chimed in with, "But keep it **small**."

The constant "suggestions" started wearing us down – or, more accurately, Chad. After dessert, we gave them all hugs and kisses and headed back to the hotel.

It was a quiet ride until Chad finally said, "You know, they made some sense. I have to report for duty. I don't even know if I'll be allowed off base right away. And I don't know anything about the Dayton area."

I just sat there in silence, my eyes welling up. As I pulled my hand away from Chad, I mumbled, "Why did we even bother to get married?"

I guess you could say that was our first disagreement, just over two days after saying, "I do." I knew Chad was right, but I was hurt. I felt betrayed, especially since he had promised we wouldn't be separated. We continued to discuss the issue at the hotel and reluctantly agreed I would stay home while he settled in Ohio. But I let him know in no uncertain terms I wasn't happy with the decision. We went to bed with a kiss and "I love you," but then simply went to sleep – or at least we pretended to sleep.

Chapter Eleven

On Tuesday, Chad headed to Ohio and I went back home. I was adamant about moving to Dayton, and I immediately started making plans. I went to my guidance counselor at school, who worked with me to find another school in Ohio, Wright State University, where my credits and clinical time could be transferred. I also learned a lot about being a military wife.

While we were 99 percent certain Chad would be assigned to Wright-Patterson, we hadn't expected him to leave right away for commissioned officer training at Maxwell Air Force Base in Alabama for six weeks. His mom, dad, brother, and I flew down for his graduation, and Chad and I us drove back to Dayton so we could do some apartment hunting. We found a nice little attic apartment just outside of the city just in time for me to rush home, pack up necessities, return, and get ready for my final years in college. It was a wild August.

Mom, of course, was livid. In fact, before I headed to Alabama, we had one of our traditional battles. How could I do this? Why was I shutting her out? What about having a church wedding? Didn't I care about anyone but myself?

When the reality of the move sunk in, Mom softened a little. Still, she stubbornly insisted we have a church wedding. Chad and I had talked about it; we were content with what we had done, but we agreed to a small gathering for family and friends over the Thanksgiving weekend. I relayed the information to Mom. I told her it was going to be small and simple, and Chad and I were just going to show up. We would be too busy to plan a formal wedding. She thought for a minute, then agreed. She and Chad's Mom would contact the church, plan the reception, and send out the invitations. All we had to worry about was the wedding party and showing up. Surprise – we ended up with a small, intimate wedding with over 250 guests! The moms had gotten carried away, although in retrospect it did turn out well. Of course, my Mom couldn't let my decision to wear my original wedding dress go without criticism.

Our first "home" was a three-room attic apartment, just big enough for the two of us. We learned so much there about each other, about ourselves, and about life in general. Chad learned a new language – "woman speak" – and expanded his vocabulary to include words like period, PMS, and cramps. He discovered Midol was a real product with a real purpose and uncovered the true meaning of mood swings. He didn't understand them, but he quickly recognized their existence. He learned what not to say (usually after it was too late, and his foot was firmly inserted into his mouth) and to always put the toilet seat down. He learned the difference between the playful and light "Chad," the are-you-kidding "Chaaaad," and the serious "Chadwick." I taught him how to eat leftovers, and we built up a tolerance for a thousand recipes with Spam. Spam and Beans with Maple Syrup was his favorite.

Chad introduced me to sleeping with the window open – even in the dead of winter – and the pure, exhilarating pleasure of waking up with snow on your nose, going to Dairy Queen during a blizzard, sleeping in the nude (although I never bought into that one), and shopping and doing laundry at three in the morning. We learned about budgeting, meal planning, bill paying, stretching paychecks, entertaining ourselves, sale searching, coupon clipping, taking naps, afternoon delight, and just plain old relaxing. We managed to do a lot together despite our crazy schedules, always starting with a cup of coffee in the morning when we could and ending with us tucking each other in at night. We were happy and comfortable in that little three-room apartment.

Our second Christmas season brought us our greatest gift. After making love, Chad stroked my hair as he loved to do and whispered excitedly, "Tonight we created a new life."

I knew it was wishful thinking, but I answered, "I know."

A few of weeks later, I was feeling blue when Chad came home and gave me a kiss. "Hi hon. You okay? You look a little down."

"I went to the doctor's today and …"

"You're pregnant?"

"Yes."

"Sweetheart, that's great." He stopped, sensing I wasn't as excited as he was. "Isn't it?"

"Of course it is. I knew I was pregnant. I could sense it."

"Okay. So why aren't you jumping for joy?"

"You spoiled the good news."

Chad had one of those confused looks on his face.

"I wanted to be the one to tell you the rabbit died," I said as I melted into his arms.

It was time to face the realities of parenthood. I mean, I was only 21, and Chad had just turned 23. What did we know about being parents?

Well, like those before us and those who will come after us, it was a learning experience on the seat of our pants. I worried about things like not having a crib. Chad worried about having another mouth to feed. But we got through it. I graduated with a little baby bump. On September 8, 1969, at 4:12 p.m., Chadwick William Watt Jr. joined the world. We opted to call him JR. My Chad wasn't a junior. His Dad was Chadwick Sheamus, named after his maternal grandfather, but he had vowed not to saddle a son with that middle name so my Chad's middle name was William to honor his maternal grandfather.

We could take JR anywhere and he would sleep. Other than during potty training, he was a perfect introduction to parenthood. Still, his arrival forced us to look for a larger two-bedroom apartment on base. Moving into the apartment marked the end of our honeymoon. When we moved out, we were starting a new beginning in our lives. I worked for a little while before JR was born, but Chad said my job was to take care of our son. I took this job seriously.

We took a vacation in 1971 to Lake George in the Adirondacks of New York. Hectic days at Frontier Town and petting zoos were capped with nights under the stars overlooking the lake. We stayed in a one room cabin, and I was busy rearranging the furniture shortly after we arrived. I moved a couple of chairs onto the porch, and that was our nightly sanctuary. I would make a pot of coffee, and we would unwind while JR slept inside. We would just sit for hours, talking about the first couple of years of our marriage and our future. We had never had a vacation that relaxing before.

I was in an upbeat mood. I thought it was the clean air, but as we were getting ready to go back home, I walked to the car with JR in my arms and gave Chad a big hug and kiss.

"Wow, what was that about?" Chad asked.

Smiling, I answered, "Can't a wife give her husband a kiss?"

"Any time!" he said as he pulled me a little closer for another kiss and group hug.

"We're going to be leaving tomorrow and I just wanted you to know how much fun I've had on this vacation."

"Yeah, you really fit in at Frontier Town."

"That shootout scared me. Didn't bother JR though."

He stroked JR's head. "He was a tough little guy. Remember when the goat started nibbling at his shorts at Adventureland?"

"Poor kid. He didn't know whether to laugh or cry."

"Yes," said Chad. "It's been a good vacation."

I gave Chad another kiss and hug. "I'm not sure, but I think I'm pregnant," I said.

His eyes widened. "Are you sure ..."

"Not sure, but pretty sure," I said with a big smile.

"Sweetheart. I love you." That prompted another big kiss.

I was, but this time it was a rough pregnancy. Chad had to go to Colorado for a few weeks. He called every night, but I never told him how I was really feeling. I had been spotting for a couple of days, but I didn't tell anyone. I didn't even call my doctor.

That changed as soon as Chad walked through the door. He immediately called my doctor and whisked me off to the emergency room. Everything seemed okay, but the doctor ordered bed rest for a couple of weeks – something nearly impossible with a two-year-old running around.

Still, we got through it, and we cried tears of joy when Katelyn Danielle Watt (Kate-D) was introduced to the world on January 25, 1972, also ironically at 4:12 a.m.

We had birthday parties and watched JR and Kate-D grow. We played cards with our neighbors, always welcoming a steady stream of friends into the apartment. Kate-D was impossible; she didn't want to sleep anywhere except in her crib, so we never went out. She was also a rocker. In fact, she put her head through the crib headboard. Meanwhile, JR was a typical toddler, getting into everything, including repainting the living room walls with butter. The two urchins wore me down.

Chad noticed a new housing development going up. He packed us up one weekend and we went to see the area. The land was just being cleared; there was only one "show home" and a couple of others under construction. We went through the figures and calculations. Since the house was under construction, we could "save" some money by not adding a gambrel roof and doing our own painting. All we needed was $7,000 down.

Chad and I went through every possible scenario to get our payments in line. If we sold the car … if we scrimped here and there … if we … I'll admit I was less enthusiastic and more realistic. If we sold the car, we would have to get another one. Even if we scrimped and saved, the pennies wouldn't add up fast enough.

Yet, somehow, the pieces fell into place. Chad was promoted in rank and pay. We found a buyer for the Chevy wagon and a reliable replacement, which meant no more car payments. We kept filling our water jug with loose change, and we culled as many extras from the house as we could, like a finished basement, painting, landscaping other than basic seeding, and the gambrel roof over the door.

The mortgage application somehow went through. We were going to be new homeowners! We closed in late 1974. After a check for the escrow … and another for the taxes … and another for the insurance … and another for the points … and another for I don't remember what, we were both in shock.

When we got back to the car, all I could ask was, "What did we just get ourselves into? Are we going to be okay?" Chad said, "Sure we are."

It all turned out fine – just don't ask me how. We managed to get some of the work done around the house. Chad was a good engineer, but he was not as handy with a hammer or screwdriver. Still, he framed a patio and had concrete poured, although it had a slight pitch. (Okay, a marble would roll right off it.) He also finished a room in the basement. (Okay, it had a gaping hole in the closet, and he never did find his hammer after putting up the wallboard.) I always teased him about being able to design detailed plans but not being able to follow them. I sure was glad he was designing and not building projects for the Air Force!

We finally got the fireplace we had to scrub when the house was built, and my forsythia twigs matured into a vibrant break on the edge of our property line. We even got a puppy, a playful Irish Setter named Harrigan, who fit right in with the family.

Chad spent a lot of time with the kids. He taught JR how to fish, usually with Kate-D tugging at his pant leg, pleading, "Can I go too, Daddy? Please!" One day I came home from shopping and found Chad sitting on the floor "drinking" tea with his four-year-old daughter. There was Little League and Brownies and boys' weekends and dance recitals.

Yet, like he had when we were dating, Chad always listened patiently to my words and my heart. He gave me his prime time, not the leftovers. He praised me. He surprised me. He continued to court me. He treated me like a queen in front of other people. Even though we were a military family, life still seemed normal. Since Chad worked on projects with mostly civilian engineers, there weren't many Air Force rules to deal with. He had most weekends and holidays off.

But one time in 1977, he and his team had to go to Schriever Air Force Base in Colorado Springs to integrate their portion of a satellite monitoring project with other teams from around the country. What was supposed to be a six-week assignment dragged to over six months. We missed being together at Thanksgiving, and it looked like we were going to miss Christmas as well.

Somehow, Chad found a friend of a friend of a friend who couldn't use their condo in Aspen over the Christmas holiday. He called and asked me if I wanted to celebrate Christmas in Colorado. I had about a million reasons why we shouldn't, but I sure did miss him, and I knew the kids did too. We thought about flying, but I decided to drive the three days and 1,200 miles with a five-year-old and an eight-year-old. It was quite an adventure, navigating unpredictable weather and trying to keep JR and Kate-D occupied, but it was worth it. They enjoyed eating out and spending nights at motels and taking in the sights as the scenery which morphed from flat farmland to colorful mountains. We played plenty of I Spy, and License Plate Bingo and they kept themselves busy coloring and chatting and making special Christmas cards for Daddy.

Chad brought a Christmas tree and decorated it, which greeted us when we arrived. We spent our days skiing, sledding, and building snowmen. We drank gallons of hot chocolate. We not only celebrated Christmas, but JR's and Kate-D's birthdays as well. At night after the kids were settled in, Chad and I snuggled in front of the fireplace (and then some). It was like a second honeymoon.

Of course, all good things come to an end, and the kids and I returned home. Chad finally made it back on Valentine's Day, holding a dozen red roses. He never ceased to amaze me.

Chapter Twelve

Later in the summer, Chad and I were in the PX military store doing some shopping. Out of the blue, he said, "Do you think we should start going to church?" Stunned, I stopped in my tracks. "What?"

"Do you think we should start going to church?" he asked again.

Knowing we had just buried his father a few weeks back after a sudden heart attack, my reaction was, "Is something wrong? Are you okay?"

"I'm fine," said Chad. "Forget it. I just thought the kids should start learning about God."

"I'm not against it. You just caught me off guard. Why don't we get a coffee and talk about it?"

We finished shopping and stopped in at a local coffee shop to continue our discussion.

"There's been a lot of conversation about church and God in the office lately and it got me to thinking. JR is almost nine and Kate-D six. I know we don't go to church, but we believe in God. We know what we believe, but what about them?"

"Sure, hon. We can go to church. That was never an issue. I just wanted to make sure you're okay, that's all. I thought it may have been a reaction to your Dad's death."

"Well, that certainly had something to do with it," he admitted, "but it feels like it's time."

Chad and I had been brought up in the church, and we were believers. But we never really practiced our faith after we got married beyond attending Christmas or Easter services and of course weddings and funerals. "Great. St. Paul's is just down the street," I offered.

But Chad caught me off guard again. "Yeah, but a couple of the guys go to Grace Community in Huber Heights. I thought we might try that. They're supposed to have a great children's program. And they say the pastor really gives you something to think about."

"Okay. Sure. When do you want to start?"

"How about tomorrow?"

"Tomorrow? Sure. What time is their service?"

"They have a few services. How about the 10:30 contemporary service?"

"You really thought this out Mr. Watt. It sounds like it's important to you. I'm good. Tomorrow's a new day for the family."

"Thanks. I want it to be important to you and the kids, too."

I was skeptical, but we packed up the kids and went to the 10:30 contemporary service on Sunday morning. The kids went off to children's church – a new concept for us – and Chad and I encountered a totally different worship experience than what we had ever experienced.

As the family gathered in the vestibule after service, Chad suggested we stop at IHOP.

JR quickly backed the idea. "Can we?" Kate-D started jumping up and down. "Yes."

"I guess we're heading to IHOP," I said, shrugging my shoulders.

Over our pancakes, we went around the table, sharing our views about the church. The kids appeared to be just as enthusiastic as I was.

Chad asked, "So what did you guys think?"

JR responded, "It was cool, dad. We had fun …" with Kate-D interrupting, "Yeah, fun."

JR gave her an annoyed look, but said he learned about Jesus. "A couple of the kids go to the same school I do. They were talking about a wanna."

Chad corrected him. "AWANA? Yes, it's a children's bible study program. I think Kate-D can go too if she wants to."

"I do, Daddy, I do," she gushed. "I had fun too. We colored pictures of Jesus and played games and had a snack."

He turned to me. "What about you Sam? What did you think?" he asked.

"I was skeptical at first. It was a totally different worship than I thought it would be, but everyone was friendly and helpful. It was casual with a message that focused on our relationship with Jesus, not a bunch of rules and regulations. It had uplifting music with horns and drums replacing the organ, not stale hymns. I left with a warm feeling."

"Well, what do you guys think? Should we come back next week?"

JR, Kate-D and I quickly raised our hands.

"Okay. And we'll make an after church stop at IHOP part of the day. Deal?"

In unison, the three of us responded, "Deal!"

Over the next few months, we got more involved at Grace with Bible studies and family-focused activities. The kids got involved in AWANA. Chad and I found new friends and a home outside of our home.

Of course, not everyone approved of our decision. Chad's mom and my dad tolerated the decision, but Mom was … well … Mom. How could I do such a thing? How could I turn away from God? What was she supposed to tell Father Pat or her friends?

Chapter Thirteen

I have to admit it, I felt a little guilty about attending Grace Community. My Catholic upbringing and desire to please Mom weighed on me ... just a little.

We always went to church as a family growing up, 8 a.m. Mass in the fifth pew, left side, Mary's side. I would get in first, followed by Mom and Dad on the aisle. Following Mass, we would go to Grandma's for doughnuts. It was the ritual.

We didn't generally pray before meals or make a nightly routine of bedtime prayers, but we did host the statue of Mary during May with regular devotions and Mom would often be seen with her rosary beads close at hand – next to the couch, in her purse. She gave me rosary beads as First Communion and Confirmation presents, although I couldn't tell you where they are now.

We weren't zealot Catholics, but practicing Catholics, with a big, old, dusty Bible in the corner of the living room. Of course, going to a Catholic grammar and high school nurtured the religious instruction and even at St. Vincent's I had a few philosophy and religion courses as part of my core studies.

I actually took my Catholic faith quite seriously. At Confirmation, we had to choose a saint to emulate. I chose St. Gemma of Saintonge, whose feast day we celebrated on my birthday. In fact, my full name is Samantha Marie Gemma. I had to research her as part of the Confirmation process. It was a sad story. A professed Christian, she was killed by her father in a Saintonge, France, prison for refusing to marry a pagan.

I do remember being inspired by her story. In fact, while we were silently praying as the bishop made his rounds, I reasoned if I was going to accept an offer from God, I should probably make sure I meant it. So I made a commitment to trust in the Lord at the ripe old age of 12. It was the first time I talked to God not in a formal prayer, but in a conversation. Even though I often strayed from those conversations, that impromptu prayer set the tone for my life. It gave me Someone to talk to no matter what … the good times and especially the rough ones.

Obviously, I wasn't always successful.

In my pre-teen days, I also considered becoming a nun. Mom was in her glory. Of course, it all changed when I got into high school and figured out boys weren't so weird.

I remember the first time I skipped Sunday Mass … and why. I was a high school senior at the time.

The Saturday before the "incident", I did go out on a date. As we sat in church, Mom turned to me and whispered, "Are you going to receive Communion?"

"What?" was all I could say.

"Well, do you have to go to Confession?"

"What? No! Why would you even ask me that?"

"Just checking, dear. Just checking."

I did receive Communion that day, although I probably shouldn't have, not because of anything I had done, but because of the feelings I was harboring toward my mother.

The following Sunday, I just refused to go to church. Mom kept telling me to hurry up and Dad knocked on my door. "Are you coming?"

"No."

"Why not?"

"Because I don't want to."

"That's not a good answer, Sam!"

"That's the best I can give you, Dad."

"Well, what's wrong?" he asked.

In a flippant tone, I blurted out, "Ask your wife."

"I'm not going to force you, Samantha, but we'll talk about this when we get back."

We did. Mom backtracked her comments – actually said she didn't remember asking me that question. I ended up being grounded for two weeks so I wouldn't have any distractions lingering into Sunday morning.

After graduation, I had a better excuse. My job at the bakery started at 7 a.m., so I couldn't make family Mass time. Sometimes, I would go to a later Mass, but more often than not I just skipped church for weeks on end. And I heard about it every time. Once you break a pattern, even a years-old pattern, it becomes easier and easier to fall away.

Chad's experience was similar. After starting college and moving to The Bronx, he found himself attending Mass less frequently. So, it was really no surprise we never put church attendance high on our must do list. We both felt we had a close relationship with God and didn't need the fellowship of a congregation.

Making the transition to Grace Community was a big step in our lives.

Chapter Fourteen

Throughout our married life, we tried to get back home at least once a year and the parents made it a point to visit us as well. We decided to make our annual pilgrimage for Easter 1979. I noticed Chad massaging his temple while he was driving.

"What's wrong?" I asked.

"Nothing. I just have a little headache. Probably from the sun and traffic."

"I think I have some aspirin in my purse. Would you like some?"

"Yeah."

A little while later I asked him if he was feeling better.

"Yes. Thanks hon."

"Do you want me to drive for awhile?"

"No. We're almost there."

When we arrived, Chad complained about a headache again. I gave him another aspirin, and all seemed well. By midweek, however, he was again complaining of a headache.

"Everything okay?" I asked as I noticed him rubbing his temple.

"Yeah. I have another headache. Do you have any aspirin?"

"Sure. Here you go."

"Thanks."

"That's pretty unusual for you. Three headaches in a week?"

"Actually, four. I had one just before we left and took some aspirin at the office," he said.

"I think maybe we should get it checked out when we get home."

"Maybe I need glasses. That would do it too. I just had my annual physical, so I don't think there's anything wrong."

Headaches were unusual for Captain Watt. He was in good shape, and he regularly passed his physicals with flying colors. Chad having multiple bouts with headaches in a week was a source of concern for me, although they weren't constant, and they were easily managed with aspirin.

"Okay. We'll call Dr. Sweet when we get home."

He agreed, and sure enough, he was now a candidate for glasses.

While Chad was picking up his glasses, I received a phone call.

"Hello."

Dr. Sweet was the caller. "Mrs. Watt?"

"Yes. Is anything wrong?"

"I don't know. While I was fitting Chad for his glasses, he started complaining of some pain behind his ear. I think you should come pick him up."

"Is he okay?"

"Yes. He's lying down right now, but says he has a real bad headache."

"Okay. I'll be right there."

I quickly made arrangements with my neighbor to watch the kids and picked up Chad at the ophthalmologist's office. As we were driving home, Chad explained Dr. Sweet just brushed the side of his head just above the ear. The casual contact resulted in an immediate, deep migraine and Dr. Sweet discovered swelling just under the hairline. "He told me it should be checked."

So we quickly made arrangements to see Dr. Cooper, our regular doctor. After examining Chad and ordering some tests, he sat us down. "Chad, Sam, something's going on. I don't like the results. I'd like you to see Dr. Walker, a neurologist. I've forwarded the results to him. He's expecting you to call."

"Is it serious?" I asked.

Dr. Cooper answered, "It might be. It might not be. Let's see what Dr. Walker has to say."

"But I'm feeling fine right now," said Chad. "It's just these silly headaches."

The doctor, trying to keep everyone calm, said, "Maybe. But something is causing these headaches. Dr. Walker can get to the bottom of it."

As soon as we got home, I called Dr. Walker to make an appointment, but that weekend – Memorial Day weekend – Chad has a seizure and was rushed to the hospital.

Shocked and trying to make sense of the events of the past few days, Chad and I were sitting in his hospital room when Dr. Walker entered the room.

"Chad, Sam. Let's go over a few things," he started.

In unison, we answered, "Okay."

"That swelling," he said, "I'm pretty sure is a glioblastoma multiforma tumor. Unfortunately, it is one of the fastest growing cancers of the brain and the most deadly and it appears to have already started to affect your brain stem."

The tears started streaming down my face. "Is he going to be okay?" I sobbed as I squeezed Chad's hand.

"Now, honey, don't worry," assured Chad, trying to calm me down, but Dr. Walker said, "Chad, she has a reason to be worried. This is serious. I've scheduled surgery for a biopsy and to see if I can remove some of the mass pressing on your brain stem."

"No. That can't be right. Chad never gets sick!" I insisted.

"We'll know better after the surgery. I have it scheduled the day after tomorrow," said Dr. Walker.

Chad asked, "Is there treatment?"

"I'll be straight with you," said the doctor. "Depending on what we find, we might try some radiotherapy. But it's not a cure all."

"You mean …" Chad half-heartedly asked. I was more blunt. "He's not going to die, is he?"

Dr. Walker shrugged his shoulders. "Can't make any promises. We'll ..."

"No! No!" I cried. Chad lifted my hand to his mouth and kissed it. "You have to make him better. I need him."

"We'll do the best we can," said Dr. Walker. "Chad's age and physical shape are a plus, but typical survival is only about a year and more likely six months. I'm so sorry."

I was in a state of panic. I had to call the parents and make arrangements for the kids. It didn't take long for them to arrive in Ohio. JR and Kate-D were lost, and there wasn't much I could do to help them. I was lost too, confused by the sudden turn of events.

Chad and I had a chance to talk and pray before he went into surgery. We walked down memory lane, and he told me he never regretted a moment of our time together.

"How are you doing?" I asked.

"I've been better. How about you?" he answered

"Me too. And the kids. They don't understand what's going on."

"Yeah, I guess we're all a little stunned."

Trying to lighten things up, Chad said, "I knew you were my soul mate the first time I talked to you in that club in New York. I told you that you were the most beautiful girl I had seen."

I reminded him he had also added "tonight."

"I may have said that, but I meant ever. You had such a special, quirky honesty about you. I fell in love you right then, right there."

"You say the sweetest things. You always know how to make a girl feel special."

 "I tried."

"No. Try. Don't give up. Don't ever give up, not on yourself, not on me, not on the kids."

"I promise," he said with tears in his eyes. He also said he was sorry.

"For what?" I asked.

"For this. For making you go through this. For everything I ever did to hurt you. I never meant to," he said.

I hushed him and held him as tight as I could amid the wires and tubing. "You … never … hurt … me ... You … always … loved … me … unconditionally," I sobbed. "Get … through … the … surgery … tomorrow ... One … day … at … a … time."

We spent a good chunk of the rest of the night reliving our lives together and even chuckled as we remembered some of our adventures. He said there was so much to be thankful for. One of the highlights, he confessed, was the Christmas trip to Colorado. "I was so glad you came out for Christmas. I missed you and the kids so much," he said.

"That sure was an adventure. Driving cross country in the winter with two kids. But you made it worth it. The Christmas Tree. The decorations. It was like a second honeymoon for us and the kids loved the snow and the skiing and sledding and building snowmen …"

"… And drinking gallons of hot chocolate!"

"Remember when we joined Grace Community?" I asked. "I thought my mom was going to have a heart attack!"

"No, it didn't go over too well with her," he said. "But she means well in her own special way."

"Of course, it wasn't as bad as when we eloped."

Chad smiled. "Yeah. I'd say we ruffled some feathers with that one. We caught everyone off guard."

"You're right. Everyone. Even Bernie and Jimmy didn't know. I never saw it coming."

"Well," said Chad. "You scared me."

"Scared you?"

"When you stopped talking to me for a couple of days, I got scared. I thought for sure I had lost you. I couldn't risk losing you forever. You were and are so important to me."

"Okay. I know it was stupid. But I thought I lost you. I thought you had your way with me and were ready to toss me aside."

Chad squeezed my hand. "I could never do that."

"I knew that in my head, but when you just left and all I could see were your taillights going down the street, I got scared and built a little wall around my heart."

Chad continued, "All I know is those three days were the longest in my life. I was a mess and completely lost. That's when I decided we just had to get married. I was going to ask you to marry me at Thanksgiving, but I couldn't wait."

"I didn't know that. Why didn't you wait until Thanksgiving?"

"I was still going to, but when I was finally able to get you to talk to me ..."

"At the diner?"

"Yeah. That's when I made the decision. Why wait? I loved you. You loved me."

"At the diner?"

"Yeah. I showed you the ring and was fully prepared to ask you to marry me. I figured we could have a small Thanksgiving wedding. You said yes and spontaneously I thought, why not do it now."

"Spontaneously? I never knew you to do anything spontaneously."

"Surprise! I knew I loved you. I knew we were meant for each other. It just seemed like the right thing to do."

"It was! I wouldn't trade a minute of our adventures ..." I said. Fixing his covers, I added, "Why don't you try and get some sleep. You have a busy day tomorrow."

Wryly he answered, "I just have to sleep."

"Are you going home?" Chad asked.

"Not on your life buddy. I'm stuck like glue with you tonight!"

"Thank you!"

I cuddled in a ball in the chair next to Chad's bed, holding his hand. Apparently, the night shift nurse came in and covered me with a blanket.

As the day dawned, Chad was prepped for surgery. I walked alongside the gurney as he was being wheeled to surgery. "Well, kiddo," I said as we reached the double door leading into the operating suite. "Here we are. Remember I love you," I told him as I gave him a kiss and watched helplessly as the mobile stretcher disappeared into the corridor.

I was in a complete fog but found myself in the quiet little chapel on the second floor. I don't know how long I was there – praying and crying, questioning and arguing with God. All I knew was I was physically and emotionally spent as the visit morphed into just quiet time – no words, no negotiations. I just sat there, mesmerized by the flickering candles.

Mom broke the silence.

"There you are," she said placing her hand on my shoulder. "The doctor is looking for you."

I started to get up when Dr. Walker walked in, still in his sweat-soaked scrubs.

"How's he doing?" I asked. Dr. Walker encouraged me to sit.

"I'll leave you two alone," Mom said, "unless you want me to stay."

"No, thanks, Mom," I answered, squeezing her hand.

Mom left and Dr. Walker sat down next to me.

As he grabbed my hand, I asked, "How's he doing?" I wasn't really sure I wanted to hear the answer.

"Not good, I'm afraid," Dr. Walker said. "The finger-like tentacles couldn't be removed and are growing into his temporal lobe, cerebellum and dangerously close to the brain stem."

"What does that mean?" I asked, probably with a quizzical look on my face.

"I'm sorry. We did everything we could," reported Dr. Walker. "He's resting. We'll see how he is when he comes out of recovery but prepare yourself. I don't think he will ever be the same."

"But, he'll make it. We'll make it. We'll work real hard," I protested.

Dr. Walker put his arm around me as I started dissolving into a puddle. "We'll keep a close eye on him," he said, "but I think we should consider palliative care."

"What's that?" I asked.

"End of life care."

As Dr. Walker left, Dad came in and just sat next to me with a firm embrace. He never said a word, just let me cry and cry until the tears were all spent and all was left were gasping sighs.

Chad wasn't Chad after the surgery. He had a hard time focusing or recognizing people and places. He didn't say much, but you could see the confusion in his eyes. Through those few days, though, he always held my hand, squeezing it between pangs of pain. He died on June 12, 1979 at 12:35 p.m., two days after our 12th anniversary, with me holding him tight and telling him, "I love you." Dr. Walker had given us six months. I had gotten 16 days.

Chapter Fifteen

I don't remember much about the calling hours or funeral. I remember keeping my children close under my wing as we greeted an endless line of visitors, but I couldn't tell you who they were or what they said. I was surprised by the number of people who showed up to pay their respects to Captain Watt, both military and civilian. He had touched so many lives. There he was, decked in his dress uniform, surreally sleeping in his high-gloss red cherry casket on almond velvet sheets. An honor guard stood at the corners, watching over my fallen hero.

Pastor Rick officiated the service and eulogized Chad. I can't remember all of what he said, but I do remember him saying a person's life is like the residue left after drinking a glass of milk. You have to really scrub it to remove its effect, he said. Otherwise, it stays on the glass. A quick rinse can't remove it. I don't remember where he was going with the analogy, but it did resonate with me. Chad's "milk" had left its mark on the world.

At the cemetery, all I could do was stare at that flag-draped casket. I don't know whether I was squeezing JR's and Kate-D's hands or if they were squeezing mine. The three of us accepted his folded flag, and even though I had been to many military funerals, the staccato of rifle volleys stunned me to my core. Maybe it was the sudden sound amid the eerie silence.

My parents and Chad's mom took the kids while I sat there for what felt like forever, not wanting to leave. The casket took on strange shapes and hues through the lens of my teary eyes. "What am I going to do now?" I asked the inanimate casket. "I don't want to leave you. Why did you leave me?"

Dad came back from the car to get me, and I completely broke down in his arms. "Come on sweetheart. It's time to go."

Through uncontrollable sobs, I shook my head. "I don't want to go. I don't ever want to go."

"I know," he said. "I know," pausing to compose himself. "But you have to be strong. You have to think about the kids. They need you."

"I know, but …" I started to say.

"I wish I had words of wisdom for you, kiddo. I'm just speechless. Everyone is in such shock and disbelief. I don't know why Chad died, but it was just his time."

That started the water works again. "This was supposed to be our time! We were supposed to grow old together …" I had to stop and catch my breath. "… watch the kids grow …" another pause, "… share our lives and dreams." Following another longer pause, I looked at Dad through the tears. "Now I have nothing but this incredible hurt in my heart."

Dad grabbed by shoulders. "Listen," he said, tightening his grip until he had my attention. "Again, I don't know what to say. I can only imagine what you're going through. But I knew Chad and he wouldn't want you to suffer like this. Go ahead and grieve. Go ahead and cry and get it all out. But celebrate what you had with Chad and see his influence through the kids. He's with you and he's with them. Always."

All I could muster was "We were supposed to live forever." Through the heaves I added, "I know it was a fairy tale, but it was my fairy tale and now it's turned into a nightmare."

Dad enveloped me in his arms, my tears soaking the lapels of his jacket. "I know. We're all here for you, Mom and Catherine. We're not going anywhere. And you have a deeper strength. You have a strong belief system. You have a God who loves you."

That was the wrong thing to say at that moment. "That's pretty hard to believe right now. Where's God? Why did He let this happen?"

In his wise way, Dad countered, "He didn't let anything happen. I don't know what His reason was, but I know He had a reason. He always has a reason." A second or two later he added, "He always has a plan."

"Well, His plan sucks!"

"Samantha!"

"Sorry Dad. Chad dies two days after our anniversary? The doctors give us six months to a year and I get sixteen days?"

"I can't explain it. I've always told you there were things you could control and there are things only God can control. This is one of those times when you have to sit back and wait on the Lord. He'll give you the answers when you're ready, when He's ready."

"I know what you're saying Dad, but my heart isn't buying it. It hurts too much."

"I know sweetheart. I know. Let's go. The kids are waiting for you."

I was still in a fog at home, politely greeting friends but wanting to be anywhere but there.

My parents and Chad's mother stayed for about a week, and we decided to let the kids go back with them. We figured the grandparents could keep them occupied while I went through the mundane chores of new widowhood. I'm still not sure if that was the right decision, for the kids or myself.

I didn't sleep well. Okay, I hardly slept at all. I didn't eat right. It was too much trouble cooking for one, or to even go to the well-stocked freezer for something quick and easy. I broke down in the silence of the house. I couldn't watch the television shows Chad and I had watched together. My first trip to the PX ended three steps inside the door. I just couldn't go on. There were many forms to be filled out, and even the simplest forms took me hours to complete. I had to focus to make sure the check for the electric company actually went into the envelope for the electric company. I cried every time I wrote a check that still had Chad's name atop mine, and I cried every time I went to the mailbox and found mail addressed to both of us. I cried whenever anything triggered a memory, and almost everything did.

I picked up the kids in mid-August. When I got to Mom and Dad's house, Mom greeted me with, "Samantha, you look like shit!"

"Thanks, Mom. I feel like shit, but I was hoping for a better greeting than that."

JR and Kate-D bolted into the living room and in unison blurted out, "Mommy! We missed you!"

"I missed you guys too," I said. I hugged them and planted individual kisses on them.

When Dad got home from work, he cradled me in his arms like he used to do when I was a little girl. "Love you, Pumpkin. Feeling better?"

"No, not really."

"I wish there was something I could do … something I could say."

"I know. I wish you could too."

All he could say was, "I love you" as he gave me a big, teary hug.

"I love you too, Dad."

When I went to Mom Watt's home, she greeted me warmly and lectured me over a cup of tea about taking care of myself. I love my mother-in-law, but all I heard was, "Blah blah blah, blah blah de blah."

I went to lunch with Bernie and Lynn, and the two of them tried desperately to get me to go down to the shore over the weekend, "just like we used to do." I declined. "There's too many memories," I told them. I don't think they understood, but they respected my decision, although Bernie stopped by Mom and Dad's a couple of times. She had been a good, close, let's-talk-over-coffee type friend for so many years.

I only stayed for a couple of days before we headed home. The kids had to get ready for school. It was a quiet ride home, with none of us talking or playing License Plate Bingo or I Spy like we generally did on car rides.

Chapter Sixteen

I don't know why I rushed home. It wasn't a home anymore, just bricks and mortar, wood and nails, a house. Even the normal commotion of two young kids couldn't penetrate the eerie silence within the walls.

I still wasn't sleeping well, and I knew we weren't eating right. It wasn't unusual for either JR or Kate-D to find me crying. I still couldn't watch television at night, and I wasn't focused enough to even read. So, I paced, puttered around the house, or sat in the darkened living room doing nothing, which would get me to thinking about Chad and all we had done and all we had planned to do, which drove me deeper into my despair.

The kids and I weren't eating right. I would often hastily make something for the kids, although it wouldn't be unusual for me to skip the meal. The kids became a bit reclusive, spending more and more time alone in their rooms.

The sad part about that period was I was in a fog. I took care of the children but wasn't fully there for them. I couldn't be. I was having a hard time getting out of bed or putting one foot in front of the other. It wasn't unusual for me to head back to bed after the kids left for school – not to necessarily sleep but more to avoid everyday tasks. I was in my darkest days, not coping any better. Often my sobs were dry, simply because I just didn't have the tears or will left. I yelled repeatedly at God – my new prayers for the season.

That all changed on September 12, three months to the day after Chad died. The night before was like so many others. For whatever reason, instead of wearing my pajamas, I had on one of Chad's old shirts; I just couldn't get rid of them. I couldn't sleep. After tossing and turning for hours, I made my way to the couch and curled up in the fetal position, covered by the

Cincinnati Bengals blanket that usually was on the back of Chad's recliner.

I dozed off into a suspended state, only half-consciously hearing Kate-D coming down the stairs and JR cautioning her, "Shh! Mommy's sleeping."

I heard cereal pouring and Kate-D asking, "Who's going to brush my hair?"

"I will," said JR as he apparently started brushing Kate-D's hair.

"Oww!" said Kate-D when JR found a knot.

"I'm sorry."

"That's okay."

The two of them blew me kisses as they left for school. After school, they returned home and found me in the same position on the couch.

"Mom? Mom? Are you okay?" I heard JR ask. I half opened my eyes to see Kate-D standing next to JR with tears streaming from her eyes.

"Mom," JR asked again, "Are you okay?

I managed to pull my arm from under the blanket. "Yes, sweetie, I'm okay."

With a quivering voice and trying to be stronger than his 10 years, JR said, "You scared us Mommy," with Kate-D echoing, "You scared us Mommy. We thought we lost you too."

JR tried to shush her, but I sat up and said, "I'm okay. I'm sorry. I didn't mean to scare you," as we rolled into a group hug, JR to my left and Kate-D to my right. "I love you. I love you," I said taking in the gravity of the moment.

"Give me a couple of minutes to get dressed then we'll go out for dinner. Where do you want to go?"

JR offered, "IHOP?"

"Yeah, IHOP. Can I have pancakes?" asked Kate-D.

"Sure!"

"And sausage?" asked Kate-D.

"Of course," I answered.

"Yeah! Just like when we used to go with Da ..."

JR cut her off. "Kate!"

But I interjected, "It's okay. Yeah, just like when we went with Daddy. Give me a couple minutes to get dressed and we'll go to IHOP ... just like the old days."

That's what we did. Breakfast for dinner. Over the pancakes and sausage, I realized how I had failed to let the kids talk about how they were feeling about Chad's death. I was so wrapped up in myself that I'd forgotten about them and their hurt and grief.

We talked about the happy times with Chad. "Remember when ..." became a common preface as they each shared stories. When we got home, we gathered around the table and talked some more. When it became too melancholic, I packed them up and we walked down the street for some ice cream. We got home, and I told them to get into their pj's and brush their teeth. I had another surprise for them. As they were getting ready for bed, I got into my pajamas as well.

When they came to kiss me goodnight, I told them we were all sleeping together in my bed. "We can talk about Daddy, about how you're feeling, about school, about anything you want," I told them. "Tonight is for you. Okay?"

They loved the idea. They snuggled with me. We shared our feelings. There were plenty of tears, but there was plenty of laughter as well. I got a front-row seat into what they were going through and how I had contributed to their angst. It wasn't always pretty.

"So, how is it going?" I asked.

Kate-D piped up, "Good. But I miss Daddy."

JR tried to stifle her. "Kate ..." but I gently told them, "No. It's okay JR. I haven't asked you guys how you're feeling about Daddy. I've been selfish. I've only been thinking about me."

With a tear in his eye, JR said, "Mom. We know you miss Dad. We miss him too."

"Yeah Mommy," parroted Kate-D.

"Well. How about we play a little game?" I said.

"What kind of game?" asked JR.

"It's called 'Remember When' like we did at dinner. We'll take turns and remember something nice about Daddy. Okay?"

Kate-D raised her hand, "Can I go first?"

"Sure, Kate," I said. "What's your happiest memory of Dad?"

"Well. I remember Daddy having a tea party with me. He always helped me dress my dolls and find my bear."

JR added, "Dad taught me how to fish and camp. I miss that."

"I miss Daddy too," said Kate-D through a frown.

"What about you, Mommy?" asked JR. "What's your best memory of Daddy?"

The question caught me off guard. "Wow! I have so many. But I think my happiest memory of Dad was the day I met him. It was special. And it was the start of our life together."

The conversation went on for hours. Kate-D exclaimed, "This is fun!"

Then JR brought me back to reality with, "We were worried about you."

"I know," I answered. "I've let you guys down. But that changes today!"

For the first time in three months, they had an opportunity to share their thoughts and feelings. Kate-D gave in first, falling asleep around eleven. JR hung on for another hour or so. Despite having knees in my back and an arm slung over my face, it was the best night's sleep I had in months.

Chapter Seventeen

The next day after I dropped the kids off at school, I stopped in at the guidance office at Wright State. I figured if I needed to move on, I should probably take a refresher nursing course and get my certification. While waiting for the guidance counselor, I picked up the local weekly newspaper sitting on one of the tables. By happenstance – although, is there ever truly happenstance? – there was an ad announcing a grief counseling series at Miami Valley Hospital, the same hospital where Chad had died.

I wasn't sure I could step back in there yet, but I also knew I couldn't go on this way. So, I jotted down the number and signed up. I had opportunities for grief counseling through the Air Force, but I knew so many military families. I didn't want to expose myself to people I knew. When I walked into the chapel for the meeting, I still wasn't sure it was the right route to go. Yet, when I looked around and saw the grief on my fellow travelers' faces and heard our grief counselor's reassuring voice, I knew I was among new-found friends.

It was painful. I was the rookie of the group – the youngest and the most recently widowed. I allowed the others to step up as I quietly listened. One woman had nursed her husband for years while he was battling cancer. Another had lost her husband to a sudden heart attack. A woman and her daughter had lost a son and brother to suicide. A man had come home from work and found his wife dead at the bottom of the stairs. When it was my turn, I offered my tale of woe, and like the others before me, I shared my story through plenty of tears.

As I drove home, it dawned on me: I was blessed. I had a chance to say good-bye, and I knew Chad hadn't suffered long.

Gail kept us on track and touched raw nerves while helping us understand the chaotic emotions we were going through. Putting on her pastoral hat, she kept reminding us about Psalm 46:10 – *Be still and know that I am God.* That's the mantra she preached, initially pointing out how incredibly confused we are at this stage in our lives. The emphasis was on *Be still.* As the weeks wore on, she changed the message ever so slightly, shifting the emphasis to *Know that I am God.* The transition was subtle yet transformative. We learned the one sentence was split into two distinct parts. Without the first, she explained, we were incapable of understanding the second. Even to this day, whenever I feel myself spinning out of control, I remember those words from Psalm 46:10, *Be still and know that I am God.*

I had to rebuild my life. I didn't want to, but I had to for the kids … and myself.

I knew I had to be re-certified if I was to continue with nursing, but I decided to take a different career path. I decided I would pursue a doctorate in physical therapy, with a concentration in pediatrics. I already had credits in anatomy, biology, general chemistry, general physics and physiology, so I was able to shave the three-year course into two. I also landed a part time job as an intake clerk with RehabCare, a local rehabilitation center.

It was a busy couple of years taking care of the kids and house, studying and working. It was also the right prescription – staying busy to allow my heart to somewhat heal.

I was fortunate to land a job in a private office specializing in pediatric, young adult and sports injury rehabilitation just before receiving my degree. So I was established professionally as JR and Kate entered their teen years.

The kids bounced back quickly. Both were active in Scouts and Awana, and as they got older, sports. Still, we all remembered Chad every opportunity we could. We visited the cemetery at least monthly, bringing him fresh flowers and whenever there was a conflict, we would stop and ask, "What would Dad do?"

Chapter Eighteen

It took me longer to let go and move on. In fact, I would say I never really moved on.

I didn't socialize very much. We attended block parties in the neighborhood, but I was a little reluctant to get too involved in church again. In fact, it wasn't unusual for me to drop the kids off at church and either pick them up afterwards or make arrangements for friends to bring them home. Even a couple of years after Chad's death I felt like a loner in the crowd, the poor widow other wives pitied, the perpetual target for matchmaking attempts.

I had a number of conversations with Pastor Rick about my frequent absences. He wasn't getting through to me. I still had this big chip on my shoulder toward God. He even called in the big guns – his wife Debbie – to try and turn me around. I was always cordial, even when she ambushed me by visiting with Jinx and Ellie, both young widows who re-immersed themselves in church life. I could relate with them, but still wasn't ready to forgive God.

It was actually a visit from my neighbor George that softened me.

George was the Scoutmaster and his son Georgie and JR were best friends. He lived just down the street. We were casual friends. His wife died about a year before Chad.

One morning there was a knock at the door. It was George. I invited him in and offered him coffee and a Danish. Over the impromptu brunch, he asked me if everything was all right. I assured him all was well with the world, but he smiled and said, "I've been there."

"Okay," I admitted with a half-forced smile, "maybe not all that well."

"What about JR? Everything okay with him? And Kate?"

I wasn't expecting that turn. "JR? Kate? Okay I think. Why?"

"Well, it was something JR said." I gave him a quizzical look. "He said he didn't want to go on to Boy Scouts."

"What? He never said that to me," I answered. "Why?"

"I don't know," George continued. "JR, Georgie and I were talking. I asked him if he filled out the Boy Scout application and he just blurted out he didn't think he would go on. He didn't give a reason. I thought I should check with you."

"I'm glad you did. This is news to me. I'll try and find out what is going through his mind," I rationed.

"I don't want to create a problem or have him feel I was pressuring him …"

"Of course not."

He continued, "JR's a good kid. He and Georgie get along very well. I try to include him in any outings we take."

"I appreciate that, George, I really do."

As he approached the door to leave, George turned back to me and grabbed my hand. "Sam, I meant what I said before. I've been there. I'm still there. I know what you're going through. If you ever want to just talk, call me."

"Thanks. I might just do that sometime."

That night at dinner, I told JR about my visit. "So, what's this I hear about you not wanting to go on to Boy Scouts?"

JR shrugged his shoulders. "It's no big deal."

"There has to be a reason," I asked. "You liked Cub Scouts, didn't you?"

"Yeah, sure. It was fun," JR answered without much emotion, but Kate, scooping up a French fry, said matter-of-factly, "It's because of Daddy."

"Kate!" he screamed. "What?" I asked.

"He misses Daddy. So do I," she said.

"Kate!" he screamed again. "What?" I asked again, not knowing whether to address him or her.

"Time out," I said trying to grasp the moment. "One at a time. Let's talk this out. JR?"

"I don't know what she's talking about," he argued, giving Kate an icy stare.

But she, just as matter-of-factly, answered, "I know you're missing Daddy. We were talking about it the other day."

"Yeah, but, you weren't supposed to blab it to Mom!"

"And why not?" I asked.

"Well, I know you're sad," he offered. "I thought I would spend more time with you."

"That's sweet, sweetheart," I answered, "but what makes you think I'm sad?"

"All you do is work. I miss your smile. I miss going places with you."

"Yeah, like IHOP," offered Kate, legs swinging and another French fry heading toward her mouth.

"Guys," I said, but at a complete loss for words. "I'm sorry. I'm so sorry."

"That's okay Mommy," said Kate.

"You need us, Mom," said JR. "More than I need Boy Scouts."

"You're right. I do need you … both of you," I softly said, "but you don't have to give up the things you love to do."

"Yeah," offered JR. "Mr. Callesto is nice and all, but he's not Dad."

"No. No. He's not," I said. "But he can do things with you I can't, like fishing …"

"And Boy Scouts," said Kate.

"And Boy Scouts." I smiled.

JR's eyes welled up, "I miss Dad so much!"

"So do I," said Kate, interloping on the moment.

I scooped them up into a bear hug. "Come here," I said, my eyes misting as well. "You guys have to tell me how you're feeling. You're my life. If you're sad, you have to let me know so we can talk it through. If something is going on in your life, you have to let me know. If something is bothering you, you have to let me know. I can't help you if I don't know what's going on. And I'm never too busy for you!" I kissed them gently on their heads. "Understand?"

They both shook their head and nuzzled as close to me as they could get. After what seemed like hours – it was probably seconds – JR whimpered, "That goes for you too, Mom. You have to tell us how you're feeling."

Ouch.

We borrowed a page from the past and spent the night together in our PJs huddled together in my bed. I told them. "Tonight is for you. Okay? We can talk about how you're feeling, about school, about Daddy, about anything you want,"

They loved the idea. They snuggled with me. We shared our feelings. There were plenty of tears, but there was plenty of laughter. I got another front-row seat into what they were going through and how I had contributed to their angst. It wasn't always pretty. But it was therapeutic and opened new lines of communication.

For the first time in two years, I admitted – to myself and to them – I still missed their father so much. But I insisted they be open and honest with me and I promised I would be open and honest with them as well.

JR decided he would join Boy Scouts. Sunday we went to church together and after Awanas and service we headed to IHOP.

.

Chapter Nineteen

I was warmly greeted after my hiatus from the pews. A lot of people came up to me to make sure I was okay. They hadn't pressured me, but one by one they assured me they had been praying for me. Jinx took me aside and confessed she knew exactly what I was feeling. She summed it best, "Only those unfortunate enough to be part of this sorority can understand." But she also told me it was faith that carried her through those dark days – not people, not sermons, not platitudes or clichés from people who don't have actual experience.

Jinx invited me to a widows' bible study, with an emphasis on the bible study. About six of us gathered in a small group discussing women of the bible. We were all widows, but more important we had to refigure who we were as women using the 12 biblical figures as guides. We always included about 15 minutes at the end of our meeting to share our individual struggles, encourage each other and, most of all, pray for each other. It was my baby step back into faith.

It was also my step back into life.

A few months later, Debbie, Pastor Rick's wife, invited me to what she called an "ecumenical breakfast." I had no idea what she was talking about or what to expect, but I agreed to go with her to this informal women's bible group. It evolved into an every Thursday morning breakfast at a restaurant just outside Dayton. Over a bottomless coffee cup and an English muffin or bacon and eggs, we shared our week's successes and failures, prayed with and for each other and dove into Scripture.

It was a remarkable group of women from different professions, from different faiths, from different experiences. We gathered together for fellowship and study. We never got hung up on denominational doctrines, although we did broach potentially explosive issues at a time when women were just finding a voice in the church.

What struck me most about this group, however, is how close we became. When I injured my back, I had visits from every one of them, either before or after surgery at home or while I was in the hospital. To this day, their names are etched on my heart – Aretha Bonjour, Meredith Goetz, Carol Gilkey, Debbie Grant, Sarah Groh, Pepper Keller, Tory Lindgren, Lysa Ludlow, Rebecca McNeil, Lisa Musser, Ellen Niday, Nicole Orcutt, Anne Rowe, Alyssa Smith, Lisa Snyder, Rhonda Weinreich.

That was my first real taste of ecumenism and it made a profound impression that colored my Christian view ever since.

It reminded me how far I had come in my faith journey. I was raised as a Catholic, but I remember as a young Girl Scout I signed up for a trip to the famous churches in New York City {and a badge} like St. Paul's Chapel, Trinity Church, the Cathedral of St. John the Divine, St. Patrick's Cathedral and others. I was excited until Sister Mary admonished me to stay out of "those" churches that weren't of the Catholic persuasion. I stayed on the bus for the first two stops but ventured with the other scouts into the rest. I actually thought the Cathedral of St. John the Divine was a Catholic church.

Guess what? The buildings didn't collapse on me. I wasn't indoctrinated. I enjoyed the architecture and was in awe of the stained-glass windows. "Those" churches weren't much different in structure and functionality than my traditional Catholic churches.

That was probably my – no, it was my first exposure outside my faith comfort zone and the first time I questioned why there were so many different denominations, although admittedly I didn't think about it much after getting back home.

Chapter Twenty

On a rainy April afternoon, I found myself knocking on George's door. He was an editor for the local newspaper. When his wife Tess got sick and needed extra care, he began writing an outdoor column, you know, hunting, fishing and other guy stuff. That allowed him some flexibility to work from home to care for Tess. The column was later syndicated.

I don't know how I got there, but all I could say to George when he opened the door was, "If you're still willing to talk, I think I'm ready."

"Sure, get in out of the rain," he said, although I know him I caught him off guard. We sat at the kitchen table with a sink full of dishes stacked in the background. "Can I get you anything? Coffee? Tea? Pop? Water?"

"No," I said sheepishly. "Maybe I should go."

"Samantha," he said, "you came here because you needed to talk. Let's talk."

So we talked. Actually, I unloaded a couple of years of grief and hurt on him, with George patiently listening, joining the conversation only to expand something or directly answer something I said. After the better part of an hour, he looked me squarely in the eyes and said, "Sam, I'm so sorry. I know how you're hurting. What I am most sorry about, however, is that it took you this long to share your hurt with me. I can relate to everything you said."

The comment reminded me of what Jinx had said. You can't truly know what another person who lost a spouse is going through unless you've experienced yourself. It's not just a sorority, though, there are plenty of men experiencing the same hurts and insecurities.

A couple of days later, George called to check on me, starting a practice that continued for years. He invited me to dinner to continue the conversation – at McDonald's because his food wasn't "always edible."

I received a call from George during the Christmas season. "Sam, what are you doing Thursday morning?" he asked, knowing my Thursdays were usually open after late nights at work Tuesday and Wednesday.

"Mmm. Nothing, George. What do you need?"

"I need to ask a favor," he replied.

"Okay, shoot."

"Mrs. Schmidt and I are dressing as Santa and Mrs. Claus, and we would like to have you join us."

"Our neighbor Mary?" I asked, with a slight hint of laughter in my voice as I conjured the sight in my mind. Mary was in her 70s and I'm sure George would need a pillow to pull off the Santa gig.

"Yeah, Mary. We were wondering if you could join us as an elf?"

The slight chuckle turned into a full roar. "Well, I guess so," I said over the snicker. "Why me?"

"We think you need it. It's time to take some risks."

"Okay. I don't have anything planned. What are you thinking?"

"Before you say yes, though, I have to tell you where we're going," George said. I figured it was for the kids at the pre-school in the neighborhood. "We're going to the hospital."

The giggle faded. I responded, "Miami Valley?" – a place I had avoided for years except for my grief counseling.

"Yeah," said George. "Is that a deal breaker?"

I hesitated a minute before saying, "No ..." As my mind raced, I quickly figured he meant visiting the children at the hospital. "It sounds like fun. It should brighten the kids' day."

"Umm," stammered George. "We're going to see the kids, but we usually see the oncology and terminal patients as well."

I exhaled deeply.

"You don't have to do it. Mary and I have been going to the hospital for a few years. We just wanted to include you this year."

"No. You're right. I have to stop avoiding the past and venture out."

Thursday, we headed to the hospital. What a sight we must have been ... a well padded Santa, Mrs. Claus in her gray cap and bright red apron carrying a basketful of homemade cookies, cupcakes and bread, and me, adorned in a bright green bodysuit complete with pointy ears popping out of my red trimmed green elf hat, red and white striped stockings, and bright yellow shoes with curled toes.

We made our rounds in the children's wing to the delight of the kids who for a few minutes at least forgot where they were. On the main floors, the mood wasn't as jovial. I knew from experience there wasn't much to smile about.

A turning point came while we were visiting the oncology department. There was one woman in particular. She had real sad eyes and bruises on her arm where the chemo cocktails were inserted. She was expressionless as we walked into and remained in the treatment area, mostly looking away. She wanted no part of these merry makers.

Something compelled George to go to this woman. He knelt down by her and grabbed her cold hand – the one not tethered to the IV bag – and simply wished her a Merry Christmas. She looked into his eyes and said there wasn't much to be merry about. He told her he understood and explained just a few years ago he had sat with his wife in that exact chair. He said he didn't know what she was going through, but he knew what he went through and she was right, it wasn't a merry time. But Christmas is a season of hope.

Her demeanor softened as she asked him how his wife was. He told her softly she had died, but the chemo "gave us a chance to squeeze out precious extra days, weeks and months." He reaffirmed he was in a new season … this Christmas season of hope … which he wanted to share with her.

Her eyes welled and a smile worked its way onto her face. She squeezed his hand and said, simply, "Thank you!" He kissed her hand and said "You're welcome. Hope and fight."

Watching that exchange touched me. I saw George in an entirely different light. I knew he special, just as Chad had been. It softened my heart.

Chapter Twenty-One

George and I became close friends. We would talk every day and encourage each other as we journeyed through life. He helped so much with JR while he was growing up and if I hinted an appliance was misbehaving, he was there with toolbox in hand within minutes. He escorted Kate-D to the Daddy-Daughter Dance and included her in activities whenever the situation warranted it.

He gave the masculine influence to both JR and Kate-D. Like me, they never looked at him as a replacement and he never expected them to. They did respect him and would seek his counsel on topics a mom wouldn't understand.

JR played football and baseball in high school, but his dream was to follow in his Dad's footsteps. While at Bowling Green, he enrolled in the Air Force ROTC program. He became a pilot who flew missions in the Gulf War.

JR married his high school sweetheart Heather and they had two daughters, Rachel and Nancy. He would be the first to tell you, his deployments cost him his marriage. He's still in the Air Force although he is doing more teaching than flying. He married Bekah and they have a son, Chad III, and a daughter, Diana.

Kate was a free-spirited girl in high school. She was a cheerleader and we developed a special bond. Kate was and is my "fixer." She spent a lot of time trying to take care of me. She liked George, but when it became obvious we would never get beyond the "friend" stage, she would try to set me up with dates with her friends' fathers or uncles.

Kate followed my nursing footsteps, although she was harder to get out of my nest. She went to Wright State but stayed at home until she got married to a fine young man, Al, at age 26 and moved to Toledo. She, too, has two children, a boy John and a girl Kathi.

George also decided, as a seasoned widow, he was going to take me under his wing to help me avoid the traps of widowhood. He was the salve that helped heal a broken heart – not repair it, not fill it, not replace it. I like to think we were helping each other get through the days of widow- and widower-hood. But deep down I knew I was the beneficiary in the relationship. We talked just about every day – if not directly, then certainly by phone and later through e-mail and messaging. I knew when something was troubling him. He knew when I got into my "moods."

There was never anything romantic between us. In fact, he made the comment to me once, "When you had the best, what's left?" That was my attitude as well.

It wasn't because we didn't at least think about it, though.

For whatever reason, one afternoon we got on the subject of wedding bands. George said he had kept his on his left ring finger for about five years. It was Tess' protection of him.

Then he said, "What about you? Why do you continue to wear your wedding ring?"

In my typical clueless reaction, I simply shrugged my shoulders and said, "I don't know. The idea never came up."

My widow in crime added, "Would you take it off?"

Continuing with my typical clueless reaction, I again simply shrugged my shoulders and said, "I don't know. I haven't given it much thought." After a pause, I added, "My fingers are a little chubbier than they were."

"We can do something about that," he countered. "Do you want to remove your wedding band?"

Again, with my typical clueless reaction, I simply shrugged my shoulders and said, "I guess so. There's no specific reason why I keep it on. I just haven't had a reason to take it off."

With that he got some waxed dental floss and started wrapping my finger tightly. Just before tucking in the end through the ring he said, "Are you sure about this?"

I guess my non-verbal communication belied my verbal "Sure, why not."

He looped the floss through the ring and started to tug, very gently and for only a fraction of a second. He stopped, looked me in the eyes, shook her head and said, "Nope. You're not ready" as he reversed the wrapping process.

"What? Wait!" I clamored.

"I see it in your eyes," he said. "Your heart is not willing to let go."

Yes, there was a part of me that was willing to let go – but it wasn't my heart. George understood.

I do remember our first kiss … our first very awkward kiss. We were watching *Ghost.* During the sultry scene where Patrick Swayze visits Molly while she was sculpting, as their muddy hands intertwined, George paused the movie and looked at me. "Just a minute," he said as he headed to the kitchen.

He returned with wet hands, stood behind me and grabbed my hands. As he interlaced his hands with mine, he gently kissed my neck. I intuitively played along, twisting my head toward him, closed my eyes and gave him a deep kiss. Within a second or two, however, I peeked through one eye to find him with his eyes wide open, more in surprise than anticipation. He pulled away. "Sorry."

I broke into a big grin. "For what?"

"I don't know what I was thinking."

"Yes, you do," I said demurely.

"Well … I … didn't mean –"

"To be so forward?"

"Yeah."

"Don't be. I kissed you back."

He hustled to the kitchen for a couple of towels and hit the play button. "I guess that just wasn't righteous, sister."

We watched the rest of the movie with my head on his shoulder and holding hands. After the kiss scene with the ghostly Sam Wheat using Oda Mae Brown's body to reconnect with Molly Jensen, I hit the pause button.

"Now I know what happened," I stated. "I didn't let Tess use my body."

"What?"

"You were kissing me," I said. "You were thinking about Tess."

"Now that's not fair," he protested, but I continued, "It's okay. Truthfully, I was thinking about Chad."

We tried again while watching *My Girl* a few years later. Vada and Thomas J. were at the lake. Vada asked why people got married and asked Thomas, "Maybe we should kiss, you know, to see what the big deal is."

George paused the movie and looked me straight in the eye. With a playful smirk on his face, he said, "Maybe we should kiss, you know, to see what the big deal is."

Feigning innocence, I responded, "But I don't know how," which of course led to a repeat of the kissing of the arms and closing of the eyes as he leaned into me for a full lip kiss. Poor George ... again! Instead of my eyes bugging out I broke into an uncontrollable laugh, prompting him into a laugh. And we sat there hugging each other as George unpaused the movie, both of us recognizing we were soul mates but not soulmates.

With those episodes out of the way, we were unencumbered and able to enjoy each other's company. We almost always went as the other's plus one to events and we often went shopping together, often walking into stores hand in hand and occasionally even stealing a light kiss. It made us feel young again.

We had so many memories over the years. He even tried to kill me ... not once but twice.

Generally, I sort of march to my own beat through life, but George was one of the few people I would actually listen to, especially after Chad died. At his insistence I started a walking regimen. I was walking around the neighborhood and even to the post office without huffing and puffing, so one Saturday spring morning I called him up and asked if he wanted to go for a walk. Sure, he said. Great idea, he said. Where do you want to go? he asked. I told him John Bryan State Park.

He hesitated for a few seconds, then said, "Are you sure?"

"It's only about a mile and a half. It shouldn't be too bad," I responded.

So, we get to the South Gorge Trail adjacent to the Little Miami River. We started walking, hand in hand at a leisurely pace, but quickly discovered the trail wasn't completely ready for Spring. It got a little muddy in spots, but it was relatively flat. All was well until we got to the end and I realized we still had to go **BACK**!

We decided to cross the river and take the Pittsburgh-Cincinnati Stagecoach Trail back. It was much steeper and rockier and we had to do some walking/jumping over small streams. I wasn't used to that type of hiking and was huffing and puffing.

George's words of encouragement? "Tess and I used to do this all the time. Sometimes I would carry Georgie on my shoulders."

At the time, I really didn't care what George and Tess did on the John Bryan trails. My legs were rubber … my mouth was parched … I had to stop about a dozen times while he danced on the trail to keep his legs moving.

That was the first time.

We also drove into Cincinnati to experience the Christmas season. We meandered our way through downtown stopping to look at the decorations in the store windows. We bought sandwiches at Ciancioli's for lunch and ate them at a nearby park before marveling at the collection of Christmas trees on the Square. We listened to live music on the street and visited the CG&E train display. Before heading back, we stopped at Shillito's Department Store to visit each of the festively decorated seven floors, plus the basement, two level street floor, balcony and garage. As we walked away, we enjoyed the roof-high Christmas lights. George was a grown-up kid!

I was fine for most of the trip, but about midday my toe started bothering me. I thought I had a pebble in my boot and stopped a couple of times to try and dislodge it. But when we got home, I discovered I had a blister on my big toe that ruptured. I needed a cane for the next two weeks just to walk.

I've always loved to shop and George was a willing partner. During one visit to the grocery store, I sort of got distracted at a sample stand. While munching on the pepperoni pizza I noticed George had kept walking … and talking, not only with his mouth but with his hands. Suddenly about a dozen or so steps up the aisle he realized he was speaking to air. He pivoted, scrunched his face and headed back in my direction, finger wagging as he scolded me … then hugged me as I promised not to do it again. After all, he wasn't the first to scold me. I had heard that speech before. From that point on, however, he tethered me to the cart like a two-year-old just to keep track of me.

And he got even. He stopped at a sample stand featuring a veggie burger. He told me it was good, but after choking it down, all I could say was it was the best sawdust I ever ate. I got that finger-wave again!

Chapter Twenty-Two

George got into a car accident in early 2014. He totaled his car when someone backed out of their driveway, hit him and forced him to flip over into a ditch. Miraculously, he wasn't severely injured, although his shoulder was never the same.

The doctors decided to shave the clavicle when they discovered the bone hadn't fused cleanly. I was the designated driver for his doctor appointments and surgery. As usual, we had a million things to talk about – work, families, latest gossip.

Since his surgery was first thing in the morning, he was discharged around noon. He said he was hungry, so we stopped at a little diner on the way home. As I talked about life in general, out of the blue he grabbed my hand. "Do you realize this is one of the only conversations we've had where you haven't mentioned Chad or I mentioned Tess?"

The comment caught me mid-bite of an onion ring. After a swallow, I tilted my head and said, "Hmm. I guess you're right."

He pulled my hand up to his lips and gently kissed it. "My job is done," he said with an air of confidence in his voice.

I offered to stay with him that night, but he deferred. "No. I'll be alright. I'll probably go to bed early."

That was the last time I talked to him. Sometime in the middle of the night, he suffered a stroke. A caregiver found him in a heap between his bed and the bathroom when she checked in around 8:30 a.m.

I visited him in the hospital, but it was rough watching this once spirited man reduced to a quasi-vegetative state. It stirred so many memories. I was happy to let the death watch continue without me. This was a time for Georgie and his family and George's two sisters.

He was in the hospital for a few days, but it was obviously just a matter of time before George crossed over. I did visit every day, sometimes for an hour, sometimes longer, sometimes for George, sometimes for his family.

He couldn't communicate very well, but before I left that Thursday afternoon – a week after his surgery – I held his hand while the family took a break. When they came back, I leaned over his bed and, with tears in my eyes, whispered, "I love you. Thank you for being you." His hand tightened around mine and I could hear him whisper, "I love you too. Thank you for being you." Whether or not he actually said those words or not is a question for the next life.

Georgie called me around 2:30 the next morning. George was gone.

I wouldn't characterize George as a religious guy. But he was always faith-filled. He saw God in the little things. He instinctively reached out as Jesus would to those hurting and lost with a kind word and a gentle touch. When he said "Thank you God and Jesus" it wasn't a catchphrase, but a prayer from the heart. He knew where he was going and this life was just temporary. He missed Tess every day. He was ready to live every day to the fullest but was not afraid of death. I know. We talked about it often.

I've learned God sends people into our lives. There is no doubt in my mind, God placed George in my world.

Chapter Twenty-Three

George's death was the first of three that rocked me over the next seven months.

Just after Christmas, I received a call from Mom. It wasn't unusual for us to call each other, but there was an urgency in her voice this time. "Samantha ..."

"Ut ohh," I instinctively thought. "This isn't good. She called me Samantha."

"I think you should come home. Dad isn't doing well."

"Mom, what happened?"

"He's back in the hospital," she said.

"Mom, what happened?" I asked again.

"He fell again, but this time he hit his head and broke some ribs. I don't know what to do," she said, breaking down a little more with each word.

"Let me get some things together," I said. "I'll leave in a little while. I'll see you tonight."

Dad had fallen just before Christmas and I made a quick trip back to New Jersey then. In fact, I was there for Christmas, although Daddy seemed in good spirits and I think appreciated the fact I was spending Christmas at home. I hadn't done that since Chad and I were first married.

It was also the first time we talked about that cryptic comment Dad made when Chad and I announced our elopement.

"So, Dad," I started, "Remember when you said you and Mom eloped? I never heard that story. What was that all about?"

Dad smiled. "A long time ago. Yes, Mom and I actually eloped before I was sent off."

Mom heard the conversation, and in her animated way, "Worst decision we ever made!"

"Now, it wasn't that bad," said Dad.

"Joe. Do you know how hard it is to have a secret and not be able to share it?"

"Well, it was a secret," Dad laughed.

"But it isn't one we should have had," countered Mom.

It seems Mom's family didn't like Dad. They thought she was too young, and he was the neighborhood slacker. Still, when the draft notice came and Dad was called up, Mom and Dad found themselves sitting on a park bench.

"I suggested we get married before I shipped out. It's that simple," said Dad.

"It wasn't simple. I was the only one who liked you," said Mom.

"So why did you agree, then?" asked Dad.

Mom smiled, "Because I liked you."

So, they got married, Dad shipped out and they spent the next two years trading letters.

"Did you at least get a honeymoon?" I asked.

"Don't get me started," said Mom with her classic hand wave.

"Well, we didn't have a honeymoon, but we did have a night," said Dad.

"Joe!" barked Mom, blushing.

"What? I think she's old enough," said Dad. "Besides she did the same thing."

"Yeah," said Mom, "but I had to live with two years of hell. I had to pretend I didn't care about you. Do you know how hard that was?"

I smiled. "Yeah, I do know how hard it is. How did your family take the news when you finally told them?"

"You remember how your Mom carried on when you made your announcement?" asked Dad.

"Joe!"

"That was nothing. I don't think your family spoke to you for what, almost a year?"

"More than that," said Mom. "They didn't trust you."

"But you did, didn't you?" offered Dad as he reached around for a kiss.

I just shook my head. "Wow. That's quite a story. I only needed 67 years to hear it!"

"How would you have felt if Kate-D ran off and eloped?" asked Mom.

"I wouldn't have liked it, but I think I would have understood, and I would have been supportive."

"Really! I don't believe it," said Mom as she walked out of the room.

Dad gave me a hug. "Ancient history."

"You always said you got married at St. Joseph's," I said.

Mom peeked in with the announcement, "We did. It was your Dad and me, Max and Jenny, my brother Dave, Dad's family and Father Michael. No flowers. No white dress. No reception. Nothing."

"We did okay, didn't we Mom?" offered Dad.

"Yeah but it would have been nice to get some flatware," countered Mom with a smile.

This latest call came just days after getting back to Ohio, but I jumped back into the car for the trip back east.

I was tired when I arrived at my childhood home. The lights were off as I fumbled for the key. "Mom? Mom?" I called out, walking to the bedroom. "Mom?" I said quietly as I saw her sleeping and pulled up a blanket.

"Samantha?" she said, partially opening her eyes. "I'm glad you came."

"Of course. So, what happened?"

"Your Dad fell and hit his head. Knocked him out. I called the ambulance and they brought him to the hospital."

"How's he doing?" I asked.

"Well, he's grumpy, so I think okay … but it scared me when I heard the thud and saw him on the floor."

"Of course. Was he out long?"

"A couple of minutes, I guess. Argued with me the whole time about calling the ambulance and making a fuss."

"Are you okay?" I asked.

"Just tired," she answered.

"Me too. Get some sleep. We'll talk in the morning."

I was shocked when we got to the hospital in the morning. Dad was pretty bruised and having a hard time breathing.

When Mom went down to the cafeteria, Dad called me close in. "You have to promise me something Sweetheart."

"Anything Daddy. You know that."

"You have to take care of Mom."

"Of course."

"No, I mean it. I know you and Mom don't always get along, but she's a good woman and she will need your help."

"Well, I know."

"Believe it or not, you two are so much alike. But she is going to need you. Give her a chance and promise me you will take care of her."

"I will, Dad. I will," but stop talking like you're not going to be around."

"I'm not," he confided, "at least not for long. They told me yesterday I'm probably going to be in a wheelchair for the rest of my life."

"Oh, Daddy," I whimpered as Mom walked back into the room.

"He told you," she motioned.

"Yes, I told her about the wheelchair," said Dad. "I don't know how you are going to take care of me. I've been taking care of you."

"I'll manage," she said abruptly.

Dad got progressively worse over the next few days. One of the ribs punctured his lung after a coughing jag, and he quickly developed pneumonia. He died a few days later. He never even made it to the wheelchair.

I helped Mom make the arrangements but couldn't help but noticed a certain detachment in her behavior. There weren't any real crying sessions – except by me – and there was this far-away look in her eyes. At first, I thought it was just steely Mom being steely Mom, but it was more than that. I just couldn't put my finger on it.

Being his organized self, most of the arrangements had already been made. He even picked out his casket in advance, with instructions on how he was to be laid to rest. It was really just a matter of plugging in dates and filling in the blanks. That, too, could have accounted for or at least contributed to Mom's aloofness.

Dad wasn't an outgoing person, but obviously touched everyone who met him. He was the epitome of commitment. He was hard working and the embodiment of blue-collar America. He wasn't a "religious" man but had a deep faith. And he did things quietly. He relished being in the background with the spotlight on others. So, I was surprised at how many came to his wake and funeral.

JR came for the funeral, hitching a ride with Kate and Al. It was good to have them around, even if they didn't know their grandfather as well as I would have liked.

There were so many stories floating around with plenty of laughter amid the tears. Through it all, Mom wasn't fully engaged. She would chime in now and then with a barb or two, but generally sat quietly by herself.

I don't ever remember a time when I was growing up when I couldn't count on Dad being there. No, we didn't have tea parties and we rarely, if ever, had one on one time. But he was there in the background shaping my life not by what he said but by what he did. I don't ever remember him getting angry and there was never any profanity spewed. Okay, maybe there was the occasional damn it or Jesus Christ, although I think the latter may have been more of a prayer for help than taking the Lord's name in vain. At any rate, the outbursts were the exception rather than the rule. In fact, my first "damn" story was him telling me when he was in France during a rainstorm during World War II and he got annoyed at the water filling the trench. He yelled out "Damn it!" And it struck him. Dam the source and stop the water.

I don't know why that story stuck with me over the years, but it somehow served as a lesson to do what has to be done, regardless of the circumstances.

Another lesson I remember came earlier when I fractured my ankle during what had been up to that time a promising dancing "career". As we left the doctor's office with my foot in a cast, my eyes welled, not because it hurt, but because my 12-year-old world had just crashed and burned. I vividly remember him putting his arm around me and telling me to be strong. This wasn't the end, he said, just another opportunity. In his own way, he taught me to face adversity not with self-pity but head on and look for ways to grow, perhaps in a different direction.

In retrospect, it wasn't much of a pep talk and definitely not one of those proverbial father-daughter moments … but at the time, it brought some sense to a 12-year-old.

One other incident stands out in my mind. I was clowning around on the stairs to the attic. Okay, I was lining up my dolls on the stairs. As I backed down after placing my Barbie doll midway up the stairs looking through the railing, I forgot about her car. I stepped right on it and fell backwards … right into the wall. There it was … a big butt hole in the wall, as visible as all get out from our living room.

Mom, of course, went crazy. What was I doing? How could I be so irresponsible. Just wait until your father comes home!

I figured for sure I was in for the same when Dad got home. I braced myself for Dad's volcano to erupt and I tried to figure out how I was going to explain **THIS**. When he came home, I just told him.

Nothing. No yelling. He just shook his head. The hole was fixed, but always remained a visible unpainted, unpapered reminder until I was just about ready to move out when Mom finally convinced Dad to re-paper the wall.

Dad's role was to be a protector and provider. He had his share of trials and disappointments, but never complained. I don't know most of them. I know Mom had a number of miscarriages, but they tried to protect me from the ugliness of the world and kept me out of the loop … and I remained their only daughter. Even Mom would only talk in generalities when I pressed her about her miscarriages. So, I probably contributed to those disappointments more than I even realized.

Throughout the years, the one constant in my life was Dad. We didn't always agree as I was growing up and, actually, after I grew up. But I knew I could always go to Dad and together we could solve anything.

I think financially he was glad I chose to commute to St. Vincent's rather than board at Notre Dame or Holy Cross, but he was disappointed when I floundered with a less than stellar academic record. While Mom complained about my dating habits, Dad also voiced concern, but always in a more reasoned way. He often had to play referee between Mom and me. He thought I was too young to get "involved" with Chad and I'm sure perplexed why I would want to get married at 20. He was not overly thrilled with the decision to move to Ohio.

But he never complained. He was supportive of every decision I made. He may not have understood and may not have made the same choices, but he recognized this was my life and he respected it. That was another lesson I learned from him and shared as my children grew and embarked on their lives.

And, of course, he had a heart of gold. Many, many, many times he bailed me out when I overextended, not only financially but by talking things through, offering options and encouraging me to keep on going.

And, it wasn't just me. He helped many in the family as well as friends. He made the world just a little bit better.

I often thought Dad and I were nothing alike. In many ways, we weren't. He was super organized. I'm not. He planned everything and didn't like surprises. I tend to wing it and treat each new day as a new adventure. He was always neat with everything in its place. Me? Well, not so much. I don't mind a little dust; at least it gives me a place to write notes to myself.

But over the years – and especially over his last few years – I realized we were so very much the same. My traits can be traced back to Dad. I discovered our mannerisms were almost identical. Our temperament. Our sense of family. Our outlook on life. Our values.

We shared the same dry, unexpected sense of humor. It wasn't unusual for him to blurt something out of the blue that lit up the room or start a muffled laugh during a serious moment. I find myself doing that as well.

Dad was the epitome of commitment. He wouldn't quit and he wouldn't let me quit.

Chapter Twenty-Four

I stayed with Mom for about a week after the funeral but honestly, I couldn't wait to get back home. In that week we hardly had any real conversations. We didn't talk about Dad. In fact, we really didn't talk about anything. We weren't disagreeing, just not communicating. One sentence answers – on both sides. Mom still often seemed to be in her own world, doing jigsaw puzzles, aimlessly watching television.

Before scooting out, I promised Mom I would be back. We could go through Dad's things then, I told her.

As I finished loading the car, Mom came out with just a sweater on in the late January Jersey winter. I led her back inside. "Come on, Mom, it's freezing out here."

Back inside, we hugged. "Be careful, Sam. Be careful."

"Of course. You going to be okay?"

"Yeah, I'm okay," she quietly said, squeezing my hand – a little out of character. "Call me when you get in."

"It will be late Mom," I started to say.

"Call me anyway … even if it's midnight."

"Okay, I will. I love you."

"I love you too. Oh, and Sam, thank you!"

"For what?

"For being here. For being here with me."

"Where else would I be?"

The short conversation lingered with me on the 615-mile trip home. Putting "I love you" and "thank you" in the same sentence sure was strange coming from Mom's lips. Why wasn't I more supportive of her? Why didn't I force conversations? Why couldn't we tell each other how much we loved each other? Why? Why? Why?

I got home around 10 p.m. and immediately called Mom. I could tell I woke her up, although she insisted, she was just "resting" on the couch. "I love you, Mom," I told her. "I love you back," she replied.

We called each other at least once a week. They were mostly short calls, just checking up on each other to make sure all was well. Mom still seemed distant, so I wasn't sure what to expect on my trip back home. I planned a week off, getting in the Friday before Mother's Day.

Chapter Twenty-Five

The black asphalt looked darker because of ominous clouds on the horizon ranging from dark gray to puffs of white. Out of the corner of my eye, I caught a glimpse of white as the sun tried to peek out from behind the clouds. It didn't succeed at first, but a ray rained into the picture, followed by a halo of rays.

As I caught the rays, my mind drifted back to a time when I drove my preschoolers to swimming practice. There was a similar canvas in the sky that day. They thought the light was heaven shining through.

It was interesting they made that connection, considering we were not a church family at the time, and I had never told them about my connection to the diffused sun's rays. It did, however, lead to a brief discussion about Jesus and heaven.

I don't know why that thought had entered my mind at this moment. My children now have children of their own, all well past preschool age, but I missed those simple times when we had special moments to be present with each other. The time spent driving my children to and from their events had been priceless. As they grew, the busyness of life seemed to intrude into our lives.

The rays disappeared as quickly as they had appeared as the clouds stitched themselves closer together, and I was once again left with just the asphalt and the clouds. The darkness sucked away the happy memories. I was driving toward the darkest patch of clouds, and I was in no hurry to return to my girlhood home. There weren't always happy memories, especially with Mom and now without Dad, and I knew I would have to face those demons again.

As I turned off the interstate, I could feel my body tense. The landscape was eerily familiar yet distinctly different. There was the corner deli, the bakery, and the bars. Some had different names now, but they were the same bars, nonetheless. The bank complex took up a square block. The cookie-cutter homes looked the same.

I pulled into the driveway, the same one I had pulled into and out of so many times, most recently a couple of months ago. I grabbed my old key and opened the front door.

"Hi, Mom," I said, spotting Mom on the couch. She looked up and nodded, then quickly looked back at her crossword puzzle. Next to her were two TV tray tables, one holding a half finished 1,000-piece forest scene jigsaw puzzle and the other the still to be placed pieces. I wasn't quite sure whether it was her grief or her disinterest in my return that had spurred her apathy.

I looked in the kitchen and saw a pile of dishes on the counter by the sink. "Maybe I'll just do some dishes."

"Whatever. Let me finish my puzzle in peace," Mom fired back. I went to the kitchen, ran some water, and placed some of the dishes in the soapy water, drifting back to the past.

All of a sudden there was a crash! I heard Mom yell out, "Shit!"

"Mom! Are you alright?" I dried my hands and rushed to the living room.

"I'm okay. I just knocked over a table and all the puzzle pieces went flying."

"Mom? Are you alright?" I asked again.

"Yes, I'm fine," she repeated as I made it to the living room. There she was, on all fours on the floor, picking up a thousand jigsaw pieces. I noticed a wet spot on her behind, shadowed by a slightly larger dried stain. I righted the tables and helped her scoop the pieces back into the box. Then, trying to be discreet and sympathetic as I helped her back to her feet, I said, "Mom, you must have spilled something. Let's …"

"Or I pissed myself again."

"Well, let's get you cleaned up. Then I'll make some tea, okay?"

"Okay," she answered as her tone softened and she squeezed my hand as we walked into the bedroom.

The bedroom. Now, Mom was never Mrs. Homemaker. Her forte was working in the kitchen. Yet, when I walked into her room, I was aghast. The bed wasn't made, there were clothes thrown on it and the floor, drawers were half opened with clothes hanging out, and shoes and slippers littered the floor. It looked more like … well … my room when I was a teenager. I guess I inherited that trait from her.

As she started changing, I went into the bathroom. The hamper was overflowing, powder was all over the floor, the shower curtain liner was all bunched up with flecks of mold in the creases, and the medicine chest was wide open.

When I got back to the kitchen to put water on for tea, I was overwhelmed by not only the dishes, glasses, and cups I had washed and dried, but also with how many more still had to be done. Where had they come from?

As Mom appeared in the kitchen and sat down at the dining room table, I hardly recognized her. How had she aged so much in just a few weeks? What was going on?

"So, how have you been?" I asked.

"It's only been a couple of weeks!" she snapped.

"Actually, Mom, it's been a couple of months. I know how things are after your spouse dies."

"I'm fine. You don't have to worry about me. I can take care of myself," she responded.

"I know you can, but I wanted you to remember I'm here for you."

"Sure. For how long?"

"Mom! As long as you need me."

"You have a life. You don't have to worry about me," she answered.

With the conversation getting tense, I got up and went to the shelves over the sink. The nurse in me led me to tackle the parade of orange bottles sitting over the sink. Most of them were probably Dad's. I figured I would weed his out and take them down to the pharmacy for disposal.

Sure enough, the first five or so were Dad's. But there were still a number of bottles left, along with aspirin and vitamins. They were for Mom. *Okay, potassium. That makes sense. After all, Mom is eighty-eight years old. Metformin. That must be for her diabetes. All right, furosemide, a diuretic. Whoa, Norvasc. I know Mom has high blood pressure, but that's a pretty potent dose. Huh? More high blood pressure meds? Lisinopril? What in the world is this? Aricept. Isn't that for dementia? When was Mom diagnosed with dementia?*

"Mom?" I asked. "Mom?"

"Yes dear?"

"Have you been taking your meds?"

"Yes."

I rechecked the bottles. The dates didn't match up with the number of pills in the bottles.

"Are you sure? I don't remember seeing you taking any pills when I was here and the –"

"You weren't here so how could you see me take my pills," she fired back, this time flicking her hand at me.

"Mom. What's going on? What are all these for?"

"I don't know. The doctor said I needed to take them, so I do."

"But do you know why?" I insisted. "Do you know what you're being treated for? What's the Aricept for? Are you being treated for dementia?"

"No! No! I forget some things sometimes. These are just to help me remember."

"Well, how are you feeling?"

Mom's voice trailed. "I'm tired ... real tired."

She also looked a little pale. I had a blood pressure cuff with me – a throwback to my nursing days when I included a stethoscope in my emergency bag along with bandages, tape, and antiseptics. Even though she balked at first, she let me take her blood pressure. Eighty-eight over fifty-two, which was too low – much too low. No wonder she looked pale and was so tired.

"Okay, on Monday I'm calling Dr. Gibson. I need to know how you're doing and what you're being treated for," I told her.

Sheepishly, she responded, "Whatever."

Chapter Twenty-Six

The next morning was Mother's Day. I was reading my devotional, which focused on Titus 2:3-5, a passage telling older women to teach what is good so they may encourage the young women to love their husbands, to love their children, to be self-controlled, chaste, good managers of the household, kind, being submissive to their husbands, so the Word of God may not be discredited. The devotional read, "The scope of what the younger women need to learn cannot be communicated in words. It is action. It is an older woman who bakes beautifully, whose garden is spectacular. It is the kind of thing that faithful living communicates. It encourages younger women more than you can know. It gives hope toward the future. It gives ideas and inspiration for what kind of women we want to be. But it gives it in a way that is discreet, that encourages without pressuring. It gives it in a way that is not an invitation to complain about your life or fuss about your children. It is encouragement in the best way, encouragement by example."

As I was reading, I heard Mom call out, "Samantha! Samantha!"

I immediately stopped and went across the hall to her room. "What's wrong, Mom?"

"I just wanted to know you were still here. I don't want to be alone. Can you sit with me?"

"Of course," I said, reaching over to give her a kiss on the cheek. "Happy Mother's Day."

"Oh, Happy Mother's Day to you, dear."

"Do you want some tea? Do you want me to make you some breakfast?"

"No, I just want you to sit with me."

"Okay," I responded, "but I am going to take your vitals. You look awfully pale." Her blood pressure was still low, and I could feel her body temperature was lower than normal. I'd seen the signs before. This wasn't going to be a long journey.

We sat there, me holding her hand for minutes, although it felt like hours. She drifted in and out of sleep.

Suddenly, out of the blue, she patted my hand and said, "Sam, I'm sorry if I ever hurt you. I love you. I have always loved you."

"Shhh," I said. "I know you've always loved me, and I've always loved you."

"But we never told each other, did we?" she said.

"I'm sorry for that."

"I am too," I answered.

"Why not?" she asked. "Why weren't we close? Why didn't we ever talk about it before?"

I crinkled my nose and simply responded, "I don't know."

Mom, despite her increasingly shallow breaths, said she wanted to make me strong and independent. "You had your dad wrapped around your little finger, and I had to be the mean mom. I had to be the one to say no."

"You weren't mean," I interjected. "But you could be hurtful, almost like my feelings didn't matter. That's what bothered me the most. I mean, I could get straight A's and you would focus on my lone B. I didn't think I was ever good enough for you," I added, my eyes tearing up. "But I always loved and respected you."

"I'm sorry, sweetheart," she said. "I tried to make you strong and independent." She tried to smile, adding, "I think I was successful. Maybe too successful. You're the strongest, most independent woman I know. And that scared me."

"I'm not that strong," I said. "I'm not independent."

"Well, I'm proud of you. You're a survivor. That's all a Mom could ask for."

She drifted off to sleep again, so I got dressed, made some tea, and warmed up a couple of muffins. I also called Dr. Gibson just to let him know what was going on. When he called back, he told me how sick she really was and said he thought I knew. I told him I had no idea; Mom never said anything. All he could say was, "Keep her comfortable."

As I walked back into her room, she half-opened her eyes. She wanted no part of the muffin, but she did drink some tea through a straw.

"I'm so tired," she said. "But I want you to just sit with me and talk to me. We missed that over the years."

"Of course. What do you want to talk about? Anything special?"

"How did you get through everything?"

"What do you mean?"

"Putting up with me while growing up. Burying ..." she said, trying to remember, "your husband ... uh. ..."

"Chad."

"Yes, Chad. I should have been there for you."

"Mom, you were there. There was nothing you or anyone could have done. I had to work through it myself. Taking care of the kids was a big help."

"How are the kids doing? JR looks just like his dad, and Kate looks just like you."

"They're doing okay. You just saw them in January at Dad's funeral."

"I know, but I didn't spend much time with them."

She put her head back and closed her eyes. "Did Kate give you trouble like you gave me?"

I laughed. "No. She wasn't as flirty as I was. But I was always a good girl. I may have pushed the envelope, but I set boundaries I wouldn't cross. That's because of you, Mom."

I told her Kate was the "fixer."

"She spent a lot of time trying to take care of me. She would try to set me up on dates with her friends' fathers or uncles."

"What about you?" Mom asked. "Why didn't you ever get re-married? Knowing how outgoing you were growing up, I thought for sure you would find someone else."

"I was never interested," I said. "Chad and I had something special. I knew it could never be replicated. I mean, I went out on a couple of dates, but it just wasn't the same."

"What about your neighbor?" she asked.

"George? He was a special friend. He lost his wife a couple months before Chad died. JR and his son, Georgie, were best friends, so George made sure he included JR in camping, Scouting, and other guy activities. He helped me around the house, and we often would accompany each other to events. Not as dates, though. We were special friends … wow … for over 30 years. He died last year, just before Dad."

"I remember you telling me about that."

"What about Ber … Bet … Betsy?" Mom asked.

"You mean Bernie?"

"Yeah," she said. "I was never sure whether she was a bad influence on you, or you were a bad influence on her."

I laughed. "Bernie and I have been tight forever! She's doing okay. She still lives here in Jersey, and she operates a hair salon. We talk all the time. In fact, we'll probably get together before I head back."

"What about your other friends?"

"I saw Betty at Dad's funeral. Lynn died a few years ago. I haven't talked to Pat in years."

"Thank you," Mom said. "This was nice. Just talking with you. Just having you here with me."

"Yes, it was nice. Why don't you rest a little? And remember, I love you."

"Okay," Mom said. "I love you too, and I'm so proud of the woman you've become."

Chapter Twenty-Seven

That was our last conversation. Shortly after noon, I felt Mom's hand go limp in mine, and I knew it was over. I lifted her up and held her in my arms. She had a smile on her face, which put a smile on my crying face. She was home, and we both were at peace.

Kate, Al and the kids came to help with the arrangements for Mom's funeral. My rock, Bernie, also was a tremendous help, especially keeping the kids occupied. JR flew in the day before the funeral.

The arrangements went smoothly. Just as he did for himself, Dad pre-arranged Mom's wake and funeral. It was again just a matter of plugging in dates and filling in the blanks. The only tricky part was getting Father Pat, an octogenarian himself, to agree to concelebrate her Mass of Christian Burial at St. James and offer the homily. Father Pat had retired years ago and was in residence at a parish about 40 miles away.

Al actually surprised me as I sat waiting for everyone to get ready for the funeral. "Mom are you okay?" he asked as he put his hand on my shoulder.

Turning around, I answered, "Yeah, why?"

"You've been through a lot, especially over the past few months. I just wanted to make sure you were okay."

"I'm okay," I assured him as I reached for his hand. "I was just thinking, I'm the matriarch now … the elder in the family. I just never thought of myself that way."

He laughed.

Kate heard the laughter and asked what was going on. "Nothing, hon," Al said. "Mom just discovered she was now the matriarch in the family."

Kate smiled, "Mom, you've always been the matriarch."

JR stumbled onto the conversation. "What's going on?"

"Mom discovered she was the matriarch of the family," offered Kate as she tied a bow in Kathi's hair.

"You just figuring that out?" quipped JR.

"Well, yeah. The matriarch is the old one in the family," I said.

"No. No. No. No," interrupted JR. "The matriarch is the wise one in the family."

"Yeah, JR's right," said Kate, quickly adding with a smile, "Did I just say that?"

John joined out family circle in his brand-new suit as I got up. We all embraced in a family bear hug. "Thanks, guys," I said. "Let's get this party started."

During his homily, Father Pat seemed to focus his attention mostly on me, with only cursory glances at the pall draped casket or the congregation. Poignantly he stared right at me. "I knew your Mom for over sixty years, first as a young priest in the parish and later returning as pastor. We were friends all that time.

"Samantha, your Mom was so very proud of you. Every Sunday she would tell me 'Sam did this' or 'Sam did that.' I watched you grow up, not only myself, but through the eyes of your mother. Even when you made questionable choices, it was your mother who defended you. She was behind you all the way from grade school, through high school and into college. She always told me what you were doing in Ohio and about your family. She may not have said it, Samantha, but she loved you so very much."

A smile appeared on my face as I looked over at the casket. I could almost see Mom smiling as well.

Kate stayed with me after the funeral to temporarily close the house. We knew we would have to come back to make arrangements to sell the house and make final decisions about what stays in the family, who gets what, making a donation pile and what has served its purpose and usefulness. We took a final inventory as we covered the furniture, adjusted the heat, and set the alarm.

On the ride back to Ohio, I thanked Kate for staying behind and helping. She politely responded, "Wouldn't have had it any other way, Mom. You know, we girls have to stick together."

"Thanks Sweetie."

It was small talk for awhile, but as we merged onto the Ohio Turnpike with the sun starting to set, Kate turned to me. "Mom, can I ask you something?"

"Sure! Anytime! Anything!"

"Mom, I've never seen you at such peace. I mean, usually comments like Father Pat's would have made you ..." her voice trailed before adding, "... uncomfortable."

I smiled. "You're right, honey. Normally, being singled out like that would have made me squirm. I may have even challenged some of those comments. But I sat with Grandma over those last hours and I knew, I just knew, Father Pat was spot on."

"I'm glad you made peace with Grandma. I know you didn't have such a great relationship with her."

"It wasn't so bad. We had our ups and downs, kinda of like you and me."

"Downs?" protested Kate in mock surprise. "We had a great relationship growing up!"

"Yes, we did, but there were those times … like when you wanted to date Billy … and stay out all night with your friends at 14 … or when I caught you smoking in the basement …"

"That wasn't me," Kate mockingly interrupted. "That was JR. I was just holding the cigarette for him."

"Yeah. Yeah. Yeah," I said. "That's why I love you guys!"

"That's why we loved you too, Mom. You were always so cool."

I squeezed her hand as we focused on the road ahead. There was a storm brewing ahead of us, but all of a sudden, a single ray of sunshine found its way through the clouds.

Kate reached out her hand, pointing to the sky. "Look, Mom. Heaven is shining through!"

"You remembered. Yes. Yes. That's heaven shining through! Isn't it hopeful?"

Chapter Twenty-Eight

Closing and selling a house is a big deal. There are so many details to work out. Of course, it's compounded when you're hundreds of miles away.

Kate and I did a pretty good job identifying things that were to stay and things that would go during our walk-through in May, but I wasn't quite sure how it would all come together. After all, this was new territory for me. I still had to find a realtor and make arrangements to come back.

I prayed about it. Looking back, I could definitely see the hand of God in the next sequence of events.

During one of our weekly conversations, Kate asked me when I was going back to, as she said, "finish the job." Out of the blue she offered to go back with me.

"The kids are off from school," she said. "We'll all go. Al can manage by himself for a week or two. It will be like a vacation for the kids."

"Okay," I said. "When?"

"How about next week? Not this week, the week after."

So, now I had a crew in place.

I hadn't hung up the phone more than ten minutes when it rang again. I figured it was Kate adding to her plan, but it was actually Bernie. She was just thinking about me, she said, and knew she had to call. We talked for quite some time and I told her about our plans. I offhandedly remarked I needed to find a realtor as well.

"Really," she said. "I might know one. I worked with her a couple of times before. She helped me find my house, then sell it, then find another one." I could hear her fumbling for something over the phone. "Here it is, Mary Bridget at Squaw Peek Realty. She was very attentive to my needs, both as buyer and seller."

Bernie gave me the number and first thing Monday morning I gave Mary Bridget a call. We talked about the house and the market and our plans. We scheduled a meeting bright and early the following Monday.

I drove to Toledo Friday afternoon, and Saturday morning Kate, the kids and I headed east playing License Plate Bingo and I Spy. We decided to stay at the house since the beds were still there. We took Sunday off, but Bernie, Kate, the kids and I started cleaning early Monday. At 10 a.m., Mary Bridget was at the door. We walked through the house and around the outside and by 11 a.m. I had signed a contract for the sale.

As we were cleaning, there was another knock on the door. There she was. Betty. She heard we were cleaning out the house and had to come over to help. Of course, that was the end of our Monday workday as the three of us shared memories with Kate, Kathi and John.

Bernie and Betty had to show the kids exactly where we were in my bedroom when I was getting ready for my first date with Chad. In minute pantomime detail, they pointed out how they made sure my clothes matched, fixed my hair, complete with an air hair spray can, and applied my makeup. I tried to explain it was all exaggerated, but my girls weren't buying it – and I don't think my daughter and grandchildren did either.

"You did what, Grandma?" was a frequent phrase heard. The sins of the matriarch reared their ugly head over a Pizza Town pizza and birch beer. Kate didn't help even though she had heard some of the stories before. She looked at the kids and playfully said, "And we thought Grandma was a saint!" I looked at Bernie and Betty and the three of us just exploded into laughter.

"Your grandmother was the ringleader of our tribe," said Betty, as the conversation aged backward to our school days. "Nobody messed with us as long as your grandmother was around."

"Wait a minute," I protested. "Bernie was the enforcer!"

"Yeah, I was," she said. "But you were the one who put them in their place. You had that way of using your sophisticated charm while twisting the knife. The other girls at Mary Help of Christians never knew what hit them."

"Get out …" I again protested with a smile. "You guys … You're killing my reputation!"

"And we won't even talk about the boys," started Betty.

"No. No, we won't," I said.

To be honest, I needed that night out with my friends and family. The past few months had aged me.

I had made arrangements with Mary Bridget to have someone come in to dust and vacuum and maintain the lawn and by Saturday we had packed the car with personal items. We had already made a Goodwill run. Bernie and Betty stopped by just before we were getting ready to leave. As we were saying our goodbyes, Mary Bridget pulled up.

"Glad I caught you," she said bounding out of her car. "I might have a buyer for you. I've talked to them and showed them some pictures. In fact, they will be here in about a half an hour. I know you want to get back to Ohio, but can you hang around for an hour or so?"

I looked at Kate. She shrugged her shoulders. "We can find something to do."

"Yeah, okay. Maybe we'll go down to the Falls or the park." Kate let Al know about the change of plans.

Bernie and Betty joined our entourage as we introduced Kate and the kids to the Great Falls. Bernie parked her station wagon in the visitor lot giving them a view of the Great Falls and explaining how Paterson was built around the electricity generated there. As we shared some of the city's history, we walked across the bridge and over the suspension bridge to the back side of the falls, giving them another perspective of the city's natural wonder. We walked over to Hinchliffe Stadium. Even though it was in disrepair, we were able to peek inside through the iron gate as I told them of the Thanksgiving Day Eastside-Central football games I went to with my dad and uncles as a kid. Dad and my uncles had graduated from Eastside. I pointed to the bleachers on the far side of the field and told them that's where we usually sat.

I noticed as we walked back, our little history trip took a little over an hour, so we decided to head back to the house. Mary Bridget was waiting for us.

"Great news," she said as I got out of the car. "They really liked the house. I didn't get an offer, but they're discussing it. I've shown them some other houses and never saw them this excited. Keep your fingers crossed!"

"That is great news. When do you think you'll know something?"

"Maybe later today or Monday."

"I can't stay ..."

"I know. That's okay. I'll just give you a call when I hear something."

"Do I have to come back for the closing?"

"No. You'll have to sign some documents, but you can sign them in Ohio, get them notarized and send them to us. The agency can represent you or recommend a closing agent or local attorney. That's totally up to you."

"What's the next step if they decide to buy?"

"Well, they will have to be approved and the bank will probably want an appraisal. But I wouldn't have shown them the house if I didn't think they would qualify."

"Okay then. I'll wait for your call."

"That's great, Mom," said Kate. She looked at her watch. "It's pretty late to get started. How about we leave in the morning?"

Bernie and Betty looked at each other then at me. "Let's celebrate!"

I cupped my hands in a quizzical manner. "Celebrate?"

"Road trip to the shore!"

"Whoa, whoa. It's almost 2 o'clock ..." but Kate intervened, "I'm in! Kids you want to go to the shore and hear some more Grandma stories?"

"But ..."

"But what?" Betty asked. "We used to do it all the time."

"Yeah, fifty years ago!"

"Fifty, five, last year. What's the difference," said Bernie. "Come on, you love the shore and the kids will too."

I admit. I didn't put up much of a fuss, just enough to mask my excitement.

Seaside Heights certainly had changed since the last time I had graced its boards. It was still rebuilding after Hurricane Sandy and a major boardwalk fire, yet it was unmistakably Seaside Heights. The smells of the boardwalk – frying steak, sausage and pepper, pizza, freshly popped popcorn – were intoxicating. The flashing lights along the boardwalk were mesmerizing. The feel of the salt air was therapeutic. The steady cadence of the ocean waves was soothing. The sound of the carousel and pings, pops and hawks of the gamers were exciting. The press of the Saturday summer night crowd was re-energizing, even if they were much smaller than I remembered.

The six of us took it all in. We pigged out on sausage and pepper sandwiches and oversized slices of pizza. We people watched. The kids got a chance to ride the carousel – okay, so did I. We spent time in the arcade, splitting into teams for a friendly Skee Ball competition. We played a round of miniature golf on the rooftops overlooking the beach and boardwalk. We laughed and talked and reminisced. And of course, we capped it all off with a Kohr's custard and a few boxes of saltwater taffy for the road. Quite a road trip to cap my last visit to New Jersey ... and my last face-to-face contact with my childhood friends.

When I got home Monday, there was a message from Mary Bridget. The couple put an offer in on the house and before summer's end, the New Jersey chapter of my life – my roots, my foundation – came to a close.

Although I hadn't lived in New Jersey since my early days as a wife, I did manage to visit at least once every year. Chad and I made it a point to visit, usually around Thanksgiving. In fact, I can only remember one year when we didn't make it. We got as far as Cleveland, slid into a rest stop sideways, had a couple of McDonald's burgers and Happy Meals, turned around and went back home. We ended up with chicken as our Thanksgiving dinner, with very few fixings.

Chapter Twenty-Nine

Even after Chad died – and even as the kids went on their own --
I kept up the tradition. So, even though I was geographically
removed from New Jersey, I always felt my heart remained in the
Garden State and I was a Jersey girl.

For most of my life, the parents also made a near annual
pilgrimage to Ohio when we caught up with what was going on
back home. Mom and Dad usually came early in the summer,
while Mom and Dad Watt visited later in the summer or early fall.

That sense of family was important to me. As the parents aged
and the kids started moving out, I changed my visit schedule …
but started a new tradition of getting my kids together for long
weekends.

My grandchildren – and often their friends – looked forward to
the prospect of "Grandma's rules", often much to the chagrin of
my children and their spouses. JR and Kate would spar like, well,
brother and sister, each trying to outdo the other with "gotchas".
JR and Kate and my daughters-in-law – yes, my ex-daughter-in-
law Heather was always included – and son-in-law would just
shake their head in disbelief with how much I would let the young
ones get away with. My answer was always, "Let them be kids."

I felt it was a great opportunity for the grandkids to get to know
each other. After all, they lived on opposite ends of the state so
they didn't have that constant connection.

This year was especially meaningful. I arranged for the
grandkids and even great-granddaughters to spend a week with
me, with Heather's daughter Lauren as a welcomed tagalong. JR
and Kate arranged their schedules to help as chaperones for
seven kids between the ages of 11 and 26 and three great-
daughters under the age of five. It was a great week.

We spent a day at the National Museum of the US Air Force –
and didn't get to see everything. JR and I were the expert "tour
guides" – me sharing stories about Grandpa Chad and JR
explaining the intricacies of the various planes. We visited the
Boonshoft Museum of Discovery, an interactive science learning
center. The younger ones really enjoyed the wildlife zoo area.
We spent some time at SunWatch Indian Village/Archaeological
Park. We did some hiking – actually strolling through --Wegerzyn
Gardens MetroPark. And we caught a show at the Dayton
Playhouse.

And we had to eat! It was such a rush when JR and Kate took
center stage as we sat at IHOP – not our original one but a new
one – sharing their experiences with their dad with a new
generation over pancakes dripping in syrup with sausage and
bacon on the side. It was good to have them all home again.

The week was capped with a gala weekend barbecue. Sausage
and peppers, hot dogs, hamburgers, cheeseburgers, grilled
potatoes, farm fresh corn on the cob, lemonade, watermelon, ice
cream. I sat in my perch in the gazebo and just took it all in. My
kids, their spouses (including ex-spouse), my six grandchildren,
my three great-grandchildren talking, running around, playing
baseball and football, eating, drinking … enjoying life. I couldn't
help but muse about how blessed I was.

That night, I was both peaceful and restless. When I went
upstairs to get ready for bed, I found one of Chad's old shirts
folded neatly in my pajama drawer. I didn't remember keeping it,
but I must have. So I decided to wear that.

I couldn't get to sleep, something unusual for me. Normally I
would be in la la land seconds after my head hit the pillow. I just
chalked it to the excitement and activity of the day.

Chapter Thirty

After tossing and turning for the better part of an hour I decided to go downstairs where I made myself a cup of tea and curled up on the couch. I put on some soft music and wrapped myself in the old, somewhat tattered Bengals blanket that still had a home in the living room after all these years.

I drifted off to sleep and dreamed of myself sitting on a bench on the boardwalk in Seaside Heights. The sky was dark with rolling clouds. The waves were anxious, pounding the pristine sand in a precise, rapid rhythm. The boardwalk was empty except for a few early morning gulls and a man standing by the rail about 100 feet away. As I huddled there, I closed my eyes, soaking in the sounds of the surf, the fresh, clean smell of the air, the feel of the salt air enveloping me in the gentle breeze.

I was thinking about how blessed my life had been. I wouldn't categorize myself as "religious", but I was comfortable with my faith. Always I sought to reflect my Christianity rather than preach it. I knew I had a friend in Jesus who always walked with me as I traveled the road of life. Sometimes – a lot of the time, actually – He carried me.

I could sense the clouds suddenly open. When I opened my eyes I saw the gray was punctuated by shades of morning pink and blue with a pure white center. You couldn't see the sun but knew it was just behind that one puffy, thin cloud. Rays shot out in all directions, one illuminating the man at the rail. I could tell he was a serviceman, but he was more of a silhouette. As he turned and came toward me, the beam of light reflected off him – from the brass emblem and glean of the bill of his hat, the medals on his chest and even the spit shine of his shoes. He came closer, within earshot.

"Good morning, sir," I said. "Another peaceful day at the beach."

"Beautiful, isn't it?" he answered.

At that moment I immediately recognized it was Chad, simply from the inflection of his voice. I still hadn't seen his face.

He reached out his hand. As our fingers touched he said, "Come. We've been waiting for you. I'm here to take you home."

I got up, speechless, and let Chad – my Chad – wrap his strong arms around me as he escorted me down the boardwalk and toward the break in the sky. I quickly realized how light I felt as we walked ever more closer to the epicenter of the cloud. More and more people showed up as we walked down the aisle of light. Mom, Dad, Dad Watt, George and Tess, aunts, uncles, cousins, friends, and a host of people I didn't know. A voice from the brightest spot in the cloud instructed me. "Turn around and see what you have accomplished."

I turned around and saw my life unfold in a puzzle-like diorama from the other side of cloud. There were the failures in act and thought mingled in with the successes in deed. There were the happy times and the sad times all revealed at the same time. The Voice added, "Well done good and faithful servant" as the entourage erupted into cheers to welcome me home.

EPILOGUE

From my new vantage point I watched as JR and Kate arrived at my house.

"Mom? Mom?" they called. "I'll check upstairs," said Kate as JR turned the corner into the living room and spotted me curled in the corner of the couch.

"Kate! Mom?" he said as he ran closer to me. Kate immediately checked for my non-existent pulse. "JR, I think she's gone," she said with tears forming in her eyes. JR lifted my lifeless body up and just held me tightly just as his Dad was holding my new life body close as we watched.

Just then, a ray of sunshine found its way through the blinds. The sliver of light picked up the dust particles in the room as it crept ever so closer toward me. The ray caught my face – still and motionless but with a smile. Kate was the first to notice it.

"JR," she said. "Look at Mom. She looks so peaceful, especially in the sunlight."

JR looked at me through his tears. "No, Kate," he said. "That's heaven shining through!"

Other titles from Higher Ground Books & Media:

Wise Up to Rise Up by Rebecca Benston

A Path to Shalom by Steen Burke

Miracles: I Love Them by Forest Godin

32 Days with Christ's Passion by Mark Etter

Knowing Affliction and Doing Recovery by John Baldasare

Out of Darkness by Stephen Bowman

Breaking the Cycle by Willie Deeanjlo White

The Real Prison Diaries by Judy Frisby

The Tin Can Gang by Chuck David

I Don't Want to Be Like You by Maryanne Christiano-Mistretta

Add these titles to your collection today!

http://www.highergroundbooksandmedia.com

Do you have a story to tell?

Higher Ground Books & Media is an independent Christian-based publisher specializing in stories of triumph! Our purpose is to empower, inspire, and educate through the sharing of personal experiences.

Please visit our website for our submission guidelines.

http://www.highergroundbooksandmedia.com

www.ingramcontent.com/pod-product-compliance
Lightning Source LLC
Chambersburg PA
CBHW020957180626
46814CB00003B/1132